MISTLETOE, MURDER & MAYHEM

A MELTING POT CAFÉ

PARANORMAL COZY MYSTERY #4

POLLY HOLMES

Western Australia

COPYRIGHT

Published by Gumnut Press
Copyright © 2021 Polly Holmes
ISBN: (Soft Cover) 978-0-6451151-6-1
(eBook) 978-0-6451151-9-2

Edited by Nas Dean (www.nasdean.com)
Proofread by Dannielle Line
Cover by Victoria Cooper
(www.thebookcoverdesigner.com)

From the Author

Hi!

Welcome back to the mysteriously wonderful world of Saltwater Cove. This series has been one of my favourite series to write so far and I can't wait to get into the next book.

I've fallen in love with the characters, the location, and the adventures that keep Evelyn and her friends entertained.

Mistletoe, Murder & Mayhem is Book #4 in The Melting Pot Café Series. It was originally written under the title A Killer Christmas List and part of the 2020 Christmas Crackers anthology.

While some of the story may be the same, I have brought it into line with the previous three books, added new content, new adventures and if you think you know who the murderer is…think again.

To keep up to date with my books, you can sign up for my newsletter here:

https://www.pollyholmesmysteries.com/

That's enough from me for now. Turn the page and dive into the magical world of Saltwater Cove.

POLLY

xxxooo

DEDICATION

For Elliot,

Your energy and zest for life is always an
inspiration.

CHAPTER ONE

"**D**oes my butt look big in this?"

I jumped at the familiar husky voice of Hannah Graverson as it rang out behind me. I spun and gasped. The picture of the pale ginger-haired beauty standing before me took my breath away.

"Oh wow, Hannah, you look…um." I paused, shaking my head, lost for words.

Hannah pretty much kept to herself working nights in the kitchen at the local pub, *The Four Brothers.* The perfect job considering the dead of night was when she came to life, literally. Yep, you guessed it, Hannah was a vampire, but not your normal blood-sucking creature. No, she was a petite bombshell who detested the scent and taste of any sort of blood thanks to her human mother. With the strength and speed of Superwoman, she was still reluctant to use her abilities in public.

Hannah, like my best friend Harriet and myself, had been volunteered to help on this year's town

Christmas Village. She lucked out and was on the gingerbread stall while Harriet and I got lumped with taking Santa photos.

We usually found Hannah clad in baggy jeans, Doc Martin boots and a non-descript T-shirt of some sort. And when she wasn't working, she was usually sleeping. That was the way she kept her life out of the eye of the town gossips. I blinked a few times, testing my focus. Maybe I imagined the attractive beauty standing before me in black skin-tight leggings, a stunning floral off the shoulder flounce top with bell sleeves that hung gracefully around her wrists. Her make-up, delicately applied, showed her long lashes off to her advantage, highlighting her deep emerald-green eyes.

My gaze ran down her petite body pausing at her black suede high-heeled ankle boots with black fur trims. Stunning in anyone's book.

Why don't I have a pair of boots like those?

"That bad huh," Hannah said. The spark in her eye faded, and she seemed to go paler if that was even possible for a vampire. "I should have known it was pointless to try." She flopped down on the fake wooden present box strategically placed beside Santa's Christmas tree. Her saddened expression spurred me into action.

"Hell no," I said, squeezing my butt next to hers on the wooden box. "You look like a model. I've just never seen you dressed like this before. I mean, you usually wear the same thing to The Four Brothers most times I've seen you there, and it's not like you go out a lot. Why the sudden change?"

Hannah's eyes widened, and she stared right through me. Her jaw dropped.

Harriet giggled and in a cheeky voice she said, "You may not have dressed like this before, but after tonight, with all the attention you'll receive from the single male species, I bet you'll be dressing like it a lot more."

"You're kidding?" Hannah shot up off the box. "That's not what I had in mind at all."

"What do you mean?" Harriet asked, taking Hannah's vacated seat next to me.

Hannah paced, her hands twisting together at her waist. Why did she look like a firecracker ready to snap? There was no one left in the Christmas Village except Harriet and me. What did she have to be nervous about?

She stopped mid-step, her shoulder length ginger-red hair momentarily froze down her back before she turned. "I don't want to draw the intentions of every single male, just one. I'm a vampire, for goodness' sake. The last thing I need is attention."

"Oh, do tell," I said, leaning forward resting my hands on my knees.

Hannah glanced down at her watch and her eyebrows raised. "Would you look at that? I had no idea that was the time." She grabbed her black woollen coat in one hand and her bag in the other.

"Hey no fair. You can't keep us hanging," blurted Harriet.

Adrenaline inched through my body as the sparkle returned to Hannah's eyes.

She huffed, her lip turning up into a smile. "Okay, okay. Mercer's nephew is coming to stay with him for a while and he arrived this morning. He'll be at the concert tonight. I just wanted to make a good impression. They say first impressions are everything."

"That's right. I remember Mercer mentioning it the last time he was in The Melting Pot. He and Aunt Edie had a right old chat about it," I said. "It seemed pretty intense, and I tried to do a casual eavesdrop, but every time I got close, they hushed or changed the subject."

"Um, Hannah," Harriet said, a cautious tone in her voice. "It's fine to say first impressions are everything, but how do you explain the fangs and pale skin, and the fact that your species drinks blood?"

"*I* don't drink blood." A tired expression graced her face, and I could tell she wasn't answering the question for the first time. "I usually just come out and say it. The same way you tell people you're a witch, but I'm quick to add the part about not drinking blood. But this time I want to make a good impression on Slade."

I pulled back. "Slade?"

She nodded. "Mercer's nephew, and since I have no family in town and I don't have any close friends, I thought I'd ask you guys what you thought before I left. Well?"

"You look perfect. I wouldn't change a thing." A warm glow filled my chest, and I engulfed her in a hug. The coolness of her icy touch squelched my warm skin until a shiver ran through my body. Rejoining Harriet on the box, another shiver ran through my torso, followed by another.

Note to self: Remember not to hug a vampire for more than a nanosecond.

"What's his story?" Harriet asked.

Hannah shrugged and slipped her arms through her jacket. "I'm not 100% sure. I just know he's staying with Mercer for a few months and will be working the bar at the pub. I offered to help Mercer handing out flyers at the concert tonight hoping that I'll be able to suss him out."

"Well, good luck. Maybe we'll run into each other." I looked at the clock on the wall above Santa's sleigh and gulped. "If we all don't get a move on, we'll miss the entire concert and that would be a disaster."

"Agreed." Hannah flung her bag over her shoulder. "Enjoy the concert ladies."

"I want updates," I answered as she headed towards the exit.

She spun on her heel and winked. "A vampire doesn't kiss and tell."

"Hey, no fair," Harriet said again as Hannah's petite figure disappeared.

I smiled and shook my head, heading back towards the Santa photo station. I tucked my camera away in my bag in between my elf ears and gingerbread cookies.

"You know, some would say this is slave labour," I said, glancing in Harriet's direction. "Aunt Edie is going to pay for volunteering us to take the annual Santa photos this year. I love Christmas as much as the next person but trading my Melting Pot Café witch uniform for a Santa's helper costume is not exactly the way I wanted to spend the week before Christmas."

Harriet cleared her throat and smiled. "I happen to think you rock the Santa helper outfit. It's not that bad. I mean, look where we get to hang out."

I paused a second and followed her gaze around the Saltwater Cove church hall. It amazed me how every year the council managed to turn our mediocre church hall into the stunning Christmas Village. Glittering colourful fairy lights hung from the roof and covered the pine tree displays. A gingerbread house took pride of place at the opposite end to Santa's Photo Booth, and it wouldn't be complete without fake snow covering the trees and the front of Santa's workshop. It had central heating, which was a bonus considering my extremities were as frozen as popsicles on my way here this morning.

That's one part of winter Hannah never has to worry about. Vampires are always cold.

"It's four days before Christmas and some of us still have shopping to do. I haven't even worked out what I'm going to get Tyler yet. I mean, what do you get your boyfriend who looks like a Greek God and is happy with just my company for Christmas?"

Harriet stared at me and promptly burst out laughing.

"You have the cutest pout, Evelyn."

Pout? I do not pout.

My jaw dropped, and I stared at my best friend. I shook my head and Harriet's infectious giggle had me joining her in no time. How can I stay mad at her? Memories flooded back reminding me of the time I nearly lost her to a crazed lunatic in a resurrection ritual. Every time I think of Halloween, icy shivers cover me from head to toe. Thank goodness this last one proved uneventful. It was one of the best Halloween celebrations I can remember, but most of all, there wasn't a dead body in sight.

"Hey, Evelyn. Where'd your mind trod off to?" Harriet asked, restacking the Santa sack full of lollies ready for tomorrow's shoot. Lollies always kept the children in order. It's amazing what bribery does.

"Oh, sorry." I shook the cobwebs from my mind. "I was just thinking about Halloween."

Harriet paused mid-handful and turned her sparkling emerald eyes on me.

"Evelyn, you have to let it go. That was so long ago now. Thanks to your quick-thinking witch skills, it all turned out okay in the end. I prefer to take the positives out of the event."

My eyebrows shot up. "Positives? Did we both live through the same Halloween where your heart was almost sacrificed in a resurrection ritual?"

"Yes, we did," she said, accompanied by an eyeroll and a huff. "But it was also the Halloween I found out I was a witch who could see the future. Tyler came home from his time in Nepal and if he hadn't, you two never would have gotten together. And don't forget Aunt Edie re-connected with Detective Huxton again and we both know how that turned out."

No sooner had my insides warmed at the memory of Aunt Edie happy in the arms of her fiancée, Detective Micah Huxton, than my blood ran cold. I remembered how close we all came to losing her at the Saltwater Cove Annual Show earlier this year. I mean who in their right mind, witch or not, would try to frame Aunt Edie for murder? A psycho witch, that's who.

It had been the worst time of my life watching evidence pile up against the woman who took me in after my parents were tragically killed. This year's annual show won't be one I forget in a hurry.

Everything was right once more in Saltwater Cove. I covered Santa's chair with Alfred's big red embroidered throw blanket.

"I'm so glad Alfred was able to play Santa again this year, aren't you?"

Harriet nodded and pulled the drawstring on Santa's sack tight. "I sure am. After he had that health scare mid-November, I wasn't sure if he was going to make Christmas, let alone play Santa. But he proved the doctors wrong. I wish Jordi were here though, then it would be the perfect Christmas."

"Yeah, me too." I was crushed when Jordi, my other best friend, broke the news she was spending Christmas with her extended family in Australia. It worked in well with the annual shapeshifter conference which is being held in Perth in the new year. I mean, Australia of all places. Why would they hold their conference in a place so far away? I hear the scenery is simply stunning and the beaches are to die for, but apparently the humidity and temperatures soar so high you can fry an egg on the bonnet of a car. So they say.

"I know she's excited to see her family again, but not too keen on the location. I mean having to go all the way to Australia," Harriet said.

Teeth pressing into my lip, I paused before speaking.

"I know. Her cousin decided it would be a great idea to have a Christmas wedding and what better way to bring a family together than at Christmas time…in Australia."

"I suppose so. Kill two birds with one stone, so to speak." The words left Harriet's lips and then the penny dropped. Jordi is a shapeshifter and shifts into the most exquisite midnight black raven. She looked up, her jaw hung low and her eyes wide. "Oh my gosh, I didn't mean that the way it came out. I would never kill a bird and I certainly didn't mean anything against Jordi."

"Of course you didn't. I guess she'll have lots to tell us when she gets back, as long as she doesn't fry in the heat."

My butt vibrated, sending a tingling sensation down my leg. Whipping out my phone, I smiled at the picture of Jordi at last year's Halloween party. "Speak of the devil."

Harriet's brow creased. "What?"

I turned the phone around and held it out towards Harriet and she smiled. "Say hi for me and tell her to get her shapeshifting butt back here as soon as she can. I miss her."

I nodded. "Hey Jordi, how's it going in Aussie land?"

"Hi Evelyn, I can't tell you how good it is to hear a familiar voice. I miss you guys so much."

The sorrowful twang in her voice tugged at my heart strings. "I know, we miss you too. How are the Christmas and wedding celebrations going?"

She huffed. "They're going all right. My mother's side of the family can be…how should I put it…a bit strange at times. Most of the guests don't know we're a shapeshifting family, which means keeping our real identities hidden. Kind of makes me, Mum and Dad the odd ones out since we normally live every day with the knowledge that everyone in Saltwater Cove knows who we are, and we can shift at any time."

"Oh dear," I said, biting my lower lip.

"Oh dear is right." Jordi's voice rose an octave or two. "But that's not the worst part."

"It's not?"

"No, it's like I've been transported to hippie land. When I agreed to come to Australia, I had no idea I was going to be swallowed up by love-hugging flower growing hippies."

"Hippies?" My jaw dropped.

"Yes, Evelyn…hippies."

"Surely they can't be that bad? Hippies are cool. I bet they've welcomed you with open arms. After all, they're your family." Jordi paused and my breath hitched. "Jordi, are you still there?"

"Yes, I'm here. We live so differently in Saltwater Cove not having to hide our magic and who we are. I guess I wasn't expecting such a change. The last time we were all together I was in primary school and hardly remember them."

"Is that why your mother was so adamant you attend this year?" I asked.

"I guess so. They may be hippies, but they're family, magical or not. I suppose sharing the love is just their way of life."

"That's the way to look at it," I said in my most reassuring upbeat voice.

"I'm sure I'll survive. I only have another week here and then it's off to Perth for the conference where I can soak up the sun and the view of the hot guys on the beautiful beaches. Not to mention sharpen up my shapeshifting skills. Besides, who knows who I'll meet at the conference. I—" She paused. "Listen, I have to go. Something about a pre-wedding bonfire or something. Say hi to everyone for me and have a great Christmas. Love you guys. I'll call you soon. Bye."

The high-pitched beeping of the dial tone confirmed she ended the call. "Well, that was a whirlwind call."

"Typical Jordi. Is everything okay?" Harriet asked.

I nodded. A hot flush worked its way up my neck to my cheeks just at the thought of the hot, dry weather. I bet my skin would shred after one day in the scorching heat. "I don't envy her. Spending her days hot, sticky, and sweaty. Yuk. Give me a snowfall any day, thank you."

"Oh, I don't know," Harriet smirked my way. "They say the men in Australia are gorgeous, suntanned and walk around the beaches in something called Budgy Smugglers."

I paused mid-movement baffled by her statement. "Budgy what?"

Harriet huffed and placed the stuffed Santa sack behind his red and gold chair. "Budgy Smugglers. They're some kind of swimwear Australian men wear but they look just like underwear." She giggled. "Imagine going swimming in your underwear for all to see."

A vision of a tanned Tyler standing on a beach dressed only in his underwear shot into my mind. His sexy six-pack and buff tanned torso on show for the whole world to see.

No thank you. That image is for my eyes only.

"I can tell you right now, if we were to visit Australia, not that I have any intention of going to Australia, but if we were, Tyler will be wearing one of those full-length wet suits." I locked my camera in the storage cupboard under the desk and pocketed the key. Then I spun and stopped when I saw Harriet standing with her arms folded across her chest and her sly grin beaming at me.

"What?"

She tapped her fingers as if I were supposed to know what she was waiting for. "You still haven't answered my question from afternoon tea?"

"And what question is that?" I asked, knowing perfectly well what she was referring to: men.

She threw her arms up in the air and flopped down on Santa's chair. My neck stiffened, and I grimaced at her. Thrusting my hands on my hips, I stood in my best annoyed Wonder Woman pose. "Harriet, I just finished covering Alfred's chair with his throw rug. Now it's going to be all squashed and out of place."

She glanced at the crumpled rug and shrugged. "I'll fix it. We're not leaving the warmth of this hall until you answer my question."

"If we don't get a wriggle on, we'll be late for the annual Christmas concert and fireworks display. We're on set-up with Aunt Edie, remember?"

She rolled her eyes. "How can I forget? I swear, I've worked the hardest this Christmas than I ever have. I thought being a witch would have more advantages."

"How so?" I asked.

Harriet brushed her hand over the plush velvet throw rug and shrugged. "I don't know, maybe I thought I'd be able to use it to my advantage more. You know…in the area of my love life perhaps."

"Harriet Oakley." I hadn't intended to have such a scolding tone to my words, but it slipped out nevertheless. "You know a witch cannot use their powers for their own gain. It's against Witch Law. The consequences could be disastrous."

She grimaced and stuck her bottom lip out. "I'm well aware of that. Aunt Edie drummed it into me not long after my powers surfaced." She sighed and gave a short huff. "I just thought I might have been able to see into my future. You know, me standing arm in arm with a gorgeous hunk of a man, staring deep into his heart-warming eyes. That sort of thing."

I giggled. "Now who has the cute pouting face?"

"Hey, that's not fair," she blurted, folding her arms across her chest. "Just because you have a boyfriend now doesn't mean the rest of us can't dream a little. And stop changing the topic, you still haven't answered my question."

Harriet stood glaring at me as though I had just told her Santa Claus was fake. After I cleared my throat, I said, "I can't wait to see Jezzamy and Talen's performance at the concert tonight. I hear they've been working on some new material," while doing my best to stare her into submission. I waited and waited and waited. Then I bit the inside of my cheek and waited some more. If I bit any harder, I'd draw blood.

"Damn girl, those focus exercises Aunt Edie's been teaching you are really working. That, and your superb acting skills."

She sat as focused as a witch performing their first spell in public. I rolled my eyes.

"Fine, what do you want to know?"

She clasped her hands together in triumph. "I want to know what it's like spending so much time with Eli at *The Melting Pot Café,* especially since you have a boyfriend now. Eli's your Guardian, Evelyn, sent to protect you so he must be watching you all the time. I mean, since the return of the evil Salis Van Der Kolt, he always seems to be near you."

The Melting Pot was Aunt Edie's witch themed café we ran together. We shared the same passion for cooking and the best part was I got to dress up as a witch every day to go to work. I totally rocked the trendy hip witch look with orange and purple striped stockings. It was one of the most popular places to eat in Saltwater Cove.

Oh, God, do we have to talk about this now?

Harriet continued, "It must be worse now since you've worked out your parents were likely murdered to protect you and the Sphere. Tyler must hate that Eli's always going to be around."

"I'm not really sure what you want me to say, Harriet." I stood composed as though her question hadn't stirred the butterflies in my stomach. It had been tough for a while dealing with two testosterone charged men looking out for my safety. Once Eli revealed himself as my Guardian against the evils of black magic that had resurfaced in Saltwater Cove, life became easier.

An icy shiver goose bumped my skin. If it weren't for Eli and his ability to materialise at just the right moment, I'd be one dead witch.

He's been in Saltwater Cove just over a year now, but I still remember the day he arrived. He appeared just before Halloween and began busking opposite The Melting Pot. When he sang, his soulful sexy voice was like the Pied Piper drawing you in to his luscious world of temptation.

Harriet was the one pouting now. "I'm surprised he's stayed single. He's caught the eye of many women in town. I thought for sure Jordi would have snapped him up by now."

In my heart, I knew Jordi only had eyes for a certain town policeman. Why she hasn't made a move since the annual show is beyond me. My core temperature was about to hit explosion point.

"What are you getting at, Harriet? What's with all the questions about Eli?"

"What? I just want to know if he's fair game?" Harriet said, holding her hands up in surrender.

I burst out laughing and threw my arms around her. "Oh Harriet, you are incorrigible. I love you."

Harriet squeezed back. "I love you too," she said.

"Come on, let's get out of here. Tyler's working on a big case with Mr Bernsteiner tonight learning surveillance techniques. I can't believe how well he's taken to the private investigator business. Mr Bernsteiner said he'll be out doing his own cases in no time."

"You sound surprised." Harriet wrapped her scarf around her neck.

I shook my head. "Not at all. I knew he could do it."

All rugged up in my soft winter woollies, I watched Harriet walk ahead of me toward the hall exit. I'd taken no more than ten steps when I jerked to a stop, hearing the rambling voice of Aunt Edie muttering a hundred miles an hour in my head.

Please don't tell me you've left the hall yet, Evelyn. I'm running so late, and Micah will be here any moment. Please tell me you are still there?

I stood with my gaze fixed on the door ahead and my mind pre-occupied with the conversation.

Calm down, Aunt Edie. Yes, Harriet and I are still here. What's the problem?

Oh, thank goodness.

Aunt Edie was on the other side of town at The Melting Pot, but I could sense her relief as though she were standing right next to me.

I sent Eli home early to get ready for the concert. Micah will be here any minute and I am far from finished and we're supposed to pick up Vivienne on the way. She's bringing the raspberry pies.

My pulse raced at the same speed she was talking. It was disorientating to say the least.

Okay, Harriet and I will swing by Vivienne's and pick her up. It's all good. You just focus on what you need to do to get there on time.

Thank you, love. Have I told you lately how much I love you?

My heart filled with love, and I smiled.

Yes, but it never gets old. I love you too. See you soon.

"Evelyn?" Harriet's voice bellowed.

I gasped, jumping six feet in the air.

"I swear I am going to have to ask Aunt Edie to include me in these conversations. What did she say?"

"Sorry, that was rude of me. I didn't mean to ignore you, but I never know when she'll pop into my head," I said, pulling my purple woollen mittens over my fingers. "She's running late and asked if we can pick up Vivienne and her raspberry pies on the way."

Harriet's eyes lit up like the twinkling fairy lights on the tree behind her. "Only if I get a pie?"

"I'm sure it can be arranged." Linking elbows together we walked out, my mind and tastebuds consumed with the sweet delicious mouth-watering taste of raspberries.

"This year, I'll be on Santa's good list for sure," I said, pulling into the Botanical Gardens carpark near the refreshments area. Thank goodness it was at the opposite end to the stage where all the preparations were currently underway. Aunt Edie had arranged to have everything pre-delivered earlier this morning, so there wasn't much to do now except sort out the hot food. A piece of cake. The annual Christmas concert was the highlight of the Saltwater Cove holiday festivities. The scent of tinsel, cinnamon, and pine trees sent my senses into Christmas overload.

It was still rug-up weather, but the cool chill had held off, which made for a perfect start to the evening. Vivienne hopped out and loaded her arms with pies.

"I don't think you would ever be on Santa's naughty list, Evelyn."

I raised my eyebrows, and the skin on my forehead tightened. "You didn't know me when I was a young rug rat. While I wasn't always naughty, I had my moments, and I gave my mum and dad a run for their money." A pang of longing stabbed my heart at the mention of my parents. I can't believe they've been gone twelve years. Twelve Christmases without them, twelve long years with a slice of my heart missing.

"Where are we supposed to meet Edith?" Vivienne asked, as she headed behind the large white tent designated for refreshments.

Harriet followed Vivienne while I locked the car and picked up the last box of pies. "I'm pretty sure over by the back of the refreshment stand."

The two turned the corner and froze in their tracks. A sudden drop in temperature danced up my spine, and I shivered.

Harriet turned, revealing a deadpan expression. "Um, Evelyn, I think you better come see this."

"What? Don't tell me Aunt Edie beat us here," I said, trudging through the freshly cut lawn to join them. The winter dew dampened the ground and my shoes were having a squash fest, leaving trampled footprints in their wake. I pulled up next to Harriet and followed their now joint gazes to the ground and gasped, the air seizing my lungs mid-breath.

My jaw dropped, and I stood staring at the pale dead body of a man, a dwarf man dressed as an elf.

CHAPTER TWO

"This is not good, not good at all." My insides turned in familiar waves of chaos as I placed the tray of pies on the refreshment table and reached for my mobile. I may not be a medical examiner, but those dark purple marks around his neck looked like ligature marks to me. Knowing Detective Huxton was with Aunt Edie, I punched in her number.

Harriet's brow crinkled like a scrunched foil chip packet and her head tilted. "Evelyn, this isn't one of the elves who works with us at the photo booth. Check out his clothes, they're totally different to the uniform. If you ask me, they look like *real* elf clothes."

An over-zealous laugh erupted from Vivienne's mouth as she continued to stare at the lifeless body. "Don't be silly. What would a real elf be doing in Saltwater Cove?"

"You mean apart from sprawled out on the ground dead?" I said flatly. My words met with matching dumbfounded looks from Vivienne and Harriet.

"Evelyn, love, we're just pulling up now. We'll be there in two shakes of a Christmas bell," Aunt Edie said, with a joyous spring in her tone.

"We have a problem. Detective Huxton should bring his pen and notepad and make his way to the refreshment stand sooner rather than later." I cringed, knowing my words shattered the joyful spirit of the evening. "Harriet, Vivienne and I have stumbled across something that will put a dampener on the evening."

"Where are you exactly?" she asked.

"Walk from the carpark to the refreshment stand at the opposite end to the stage and you'll find us near the back." After saying goodbye, I popped my phone back in my bag and turned to Harriet and Vivienne, who were still staring at the body. The blood had drained from Vivienne's face. Her pale cheeks matched the colour of the fake snow back at the church hall.

"Vivienne, how about you let me take those pies from you," I said, relieving her of the trays and passing them to Harriet. Her eyes glazed over, and I feared she was about thirty seconds away from face-planting next to the dead body. Either that, or she'd throw up all over the corpse and Detective Huxton would not be happy if his crime scene was contaminated.

My pulse raced, and I elbowed Harriet in the ribs. She gasped and made an 'O' shape with her lips, her eyes glaring at me. "Harriet, put the pies down and grab a chair for Vivienne…Now. Hurry up."

Harriet's expression screamed confusion. I nodded toward Vivienne's swaying body and the penny dropped. She bolted toward the refreshment stand and dumped the pies on the counter. She grabbed a chair and shoved it behind Vivienne.

I held Vivienne's arm and Harriet took the other just in time as her knees gave way. I crouched down in front of her, blocking the view of the body. Focusing on Vivienne, I glued my eyes on hers and monitored her breathing.

"It's okay. You'll be fine. Deep breaths. In through the nose and out through the mouth." I paced my breaths to match hers, the cool evening air biting my throat with each breath.

Minutes ticked over and a rosy glow crept up her cheeks and a glint of life returned to her coffee brown eyes.

"Oh my," Vivienne said, as she wiped her forehead with the back of her hand. "That was totally unexpected. I'm not used to seeing dead bodies."

"I think you handled it pretty well. Way better than the first dead body I saw. I was a blubbering mess," Harriet said, an encouraging warm smile directed Vivienne's way. "It's not every day you see a dead body, although I've had my fair share of them.

I'd be happy never to see another one as long as I live, especially one dressed as an elf. I mean…" She stopped mid-sentence.

"You mean what?" I asked, keeping my eyes on Vivienne as her colour continued to improve. "Harriet? You mean what?"

I glanced up and a thick layer of sweat coated Harriet's brow. Her glassy eyes stared straight ahead, with the whites starkly bright against her emerald pupils. "Oh no, why do you have to have a vison right this very second?"

Since Harriet discovered she was a witch, Aunt Edie has done wonders in helping her channel and focus her visions. The telltale signs of a vision were all present, including my rising blood pressure. Harriet was a fast learner and had gotten most of the signs under control, that is, the placid ones. But Aunt Edie was adamant we let them play out. I glanced at Vivienne and asked, "Do you think you're okay now?"

She nodded and took a sideways glance at Harriet. "Yes, fine. Thank you, Evelyn, but I'm not so sure about Harriet."

I stood, and the cool air stabbed my knees, cramping them in place.

Ouch. Remind me not to crouch down in the cold again. My knees can only handle so much torture.

I shook the pain out and headed toward Harriet, stopping in front of her. I waited for her vision to finish. My chest tightened as each second passed. A stream of tears trickled down her cheeks and I could see her internal struggle to keep her hands from shaking.

"Come on, Harriet, it's time to come out of it," I whispered under my breath.

"Evelyn?" The wavering voice of Aunt Edie called from behind, but I kept my focus on Harriet. It was as if the chime of Aunt Edie's voice snapped her back to the present. Harriet gasped, one hand clutched her chest, and the other flew out, grabbing onto my shoulder and she panted.

"Oh my God," Harriet blurted, sucking in deep breaths.

She squeezed my shoulder for support, and I winced at her tight grip.

"It was awful…just awful."

"What was?" Detective Huxton asked, in his usual deep manly tone.

I spun and saw Aunt Edie standing next to Vivienne, concern etched in her expression. She was rugged up in her favourite ruby red winter coat and matching scarf. Detective Huxton stood by the body, his long Sherlock Holmes looking coat sufficiently covering his winter woollies, his notebook already out and open. He rubbed the back of his neck and his gaze drilled into Harriet. He repeated.

"What was?"

"The children," Harriet said, wiping the tears from her damp cheeks with her sweater sleeve.

The children? What children? We don't know any children, except the ones who visit The Melting Pot and mostly with their parents.

"The children?" Aunt Edie and Vivienne said in unison.

Harriet nodded, her breathing almost returned to normal. "All the crying children."

Even I was baffled. Detective Huxton ran a hand through his hair and shook his head.

"Am I missing something here?"

"I'm sorry," Harriet said, a frown marring her expression. "It was the strangest vision I've had so far. Children everywhere, crying their eyes out. In their beds, cuddled in their mother's and father's arms, in front of Christmas trees. It was awful watching their hearts breaking."

"Why were they crying?" I asked.

She shrugged. "I have no idea. That's all I could see. But I'm guessing it has something to do with Christmas."

A frigid gust of wind picked up and whistled through the pine trees, sending cold shivers shooting through my body. I swear the trees agreed with Harriet.

"I've called it in." Detective Huxton bent down to take a closer look at the ligature marks around the neck. "Do either of you know the victim?"

I pressed my lips together and shook my head. "I've never seen him before."

Vivienne shook her head. Aunt Edie squinted and leaned in for a closer look. "No, can't say I've seen him in The Melting Pot, or around town for that matter. He may just be visiting for the concert this evening."

Detective Huxton glanced my way with his eyebrow raised. "Harriet?"

"Nope," Harriet said. "But I did notice his outfit is different to the elves we have helping out on the Santa Photo Booth or any of them helping with the Christmas display in the church hall. Maybe he's a real elf."

"That's the second time you've mentioned a real elf," Vivienne said, standing, her legs still a little shaky. "I know our town is full of magical wonder, but do you really think a real elf would be in Saltwater Cove? I mean, anyone can dress as an elf at Christmas time. I just don't get why you think he's a real elf."

Aunt Edie dipped her head to the side. "Stranger things have happened."

Detective Huxton grunted and tucked his notebook back in his jacket pocket. "A dead body certainly spoils the evening and now, as this is a crime scene, the concert will have to be cancelled."

"Surely not," Aunt Edie said, with a mortified gasp. "Can't we come to some arrangement? This is one of our most treasured events of the Christmas calendar. It has been the talk of the town for the last month, not to mention the money it brings in from the visiting tourists. If you cancel it with such late notice, you are going to cause a town uproar. You could have a rebellion on your hands if you're not careful."

Vivienne piped up. "Not to mention alerting the killer to the fact the body has been discovered."

"Vivienne's right," I said, my interest piqued at the thought of keeping the killer in the dark.

"I am?" she said, her eyebrows raised.

"Yes, and at present it's only the five of us and whoever you have told at the station who knows about the body. You never know, if we keep the concert going, the killer may slip up or wonder why the body hasn't been reported and start snooping."

As quickly as Detective Huxton's face fell, he regained his composure and opened his mouth to speak, beaten only by Aunt Edie's quick wit.

She folded her arms across her chest. "Fiancée or not, I'd hate to see you on the end of a town riot. I'm not sure the Saltwater Cove police department is trained for such an outbreak." She pulled her coat sleeve up and glanced at her watch. "We've still got plenty of time to relocate the refreshment area before any guests are due to arrive. I'm sure I can whip up an additional Christmas display to keep prying eyes away from the area so you can work the scene. What do you say, Micah?"

We all waited, and I could visualise the clogs in action as he churned the suggestions over in his mind. He sighed. "Judy Rafferty, the medical examiner is on leave so I'll have to call in Irene Tammen to do the autopsy. By the time she gets here tomorrow it will be mid-morning."

He turned and looked directly at Aunt Edie. "You'll have to attend the concert without me as I'll need to be here. And I intend to be in extra early to get a head start on the investigation. Back up will be here soon to get the body and if you can erect a barrier around the crime scene, I'm happy for the concert to go ahead. But we'll all need to help rearrange things to make it happen without disturbing the area."

Aunt Edie went to work magically creating a visual spectacle of Santa's toy shop blocking the crime scene from view. I so loved to watch her work her magic. She made it look so easy. I watched as her hands swished around above her head like they were dancing their own private ballet. Exquisite and refined.

By the time we finished rearranging things according to Detective Huxton's wishes, I thought my arms would drop off from exhaustion. It was the middle of winter and I had sweat running down my neck like a dribbling faucet. I knew I should have taken my sweater off before I started.

I turned to see Harriet flop in a nearby chair. "Remind me to forgo my gym workout for the rest of the holidays. I think I just completed it all in the last hour. Gosh, that man's a slave driver. Surely there are laws against slave labour?"

"I'm with you," I said, joining her on a nearby chair; a huge exhale clearing my lungs. As hot as my body temperature was, a cold shiver scampered up the base of my neck and my body goose bumped in response. A vague memory sprung into my mind of a similar sensation I experienced over a decade ago when my parents had passed away.

Harriet bounded from her chair and straightened the lapel on her woollen coat. "I'm going to head over and see how Vivienne and Aunt Edie are going at the new refreshment stand and see if they need a hand before the onslaught of party goers. You coming?"

I glanced up at her rosy cheeks and wondered how she recovered so quickly. My muscles still ached in places I never knew existed.

"Sure. You head over and I'll be there in a minute. I just want to try and give Tyler a call."

She pursed her lips. "Do you really think that's wise?"

"What do you mean?"

She rolled her eyes and shook her head. "You said he was on a big case tonight with Mr Bernsteiner, doing surveillance or something. How would it be if you ring him right in the middle of it and you blow it for him? He's not exactly going to be happy."

I bit my bottom lip. "I guess you're right."

"Of course, I am." She beamed a huge smile my way. "Catch you later."

I watched Harriet bounce with each step and a smile warmed my heart.

How that woman has so much energy?

I begrudgingly hoisted myself off the chair and followed Harriet. A glimpse of a familiar figure to my right caught my eye, and I paused, searching for the unusual disturbance.

Nothing.

Shaking my head, I kept walking. A sense of Deja vu washed over me. I stopped and scanned the area once again.

"What is going on?" I gasped as a small, familiar woman darted behind one of the decorated

Christmas trees. I blinked several times to clear the cobwebs and looked again. Sure enough, the woman darted like a speeding arrow around another smaller Christmas tree and disappeared just as quickly.

Trixie? It can't be. Why am I seeing my imaginary childhood friend running around Saltwater Cove? After all, I made her up...didn't I?

My breath hitched, and my feet moved double time toward the tree.

"Trixie? Is that you?" I called, looking behind the pine tree. Nothing except for freshly trampled snow. I rolled my eyes and playfully slapped my forehead. "Duh, of course not. She's imaginary."

I turned and cringed as the pine needles jabbed the back of my hand.

"Aww, great," I said, rubbing soothing circles on the tender skin. I resumed my trek to the refreshment stand and my chest tightened as my gaze caught the same woman heading away from the gardens and along the esplanade toward Dead Man's Creek.

"It is Trixie, but how can it be? I swear I'm going crazy," I muttered, bolting after her. One block over and I'd almost caught up to her. The drumming beat of my pulse pounded my head but giving up the chase was not an option. She turned the corner towards Swallows Bridge, and it must have been less than thirty seconds before I turned the same corner and stopped.

Panting, I heaved in deep breaths ignoring the burn that rode up from my chest to my throat. "Where did she go? She can't have disappeared." I spun 360 degrees and ran a hand through my hair. It baffled me how she could have disappeared, unless there was dark magic at play which wouldn't surprise me in the least. The resurfacing of Salis Van Der Kolt had disturbed the balance of Saltwater Cove. And not in a good way.

I stood with my hands on my hips, shaking my head and watching the gathering town folk head towards the esplanade. They were laden with picnic baskets and folding chairs all rugged up for the concert.

"If it wasn't Trixie, then it sure as hell was her doppelgänger."

CHAPTER THREE

My body lay snuggled under the feather doona and although my muscles seemed relaxed, my head was running through the events of last night like a broken record. The memory stuck in the back of my mind, just out of reach.

My lungs burned, and I caught sight of Trixie once more. Scorching heat inched through my chest like a hot witch's cauldron coming to the boil. "Trixie…Trixie," I called at the top of my lungs. Why couldn't she hear me? My legs wobbled and my whole body was seconds from exploding from exhaustion. I gasped and panted, praying she'd turn around before I collapsed into a heap on the pavement.

I failed. She was gone. Heaving and puffing, I spun and headed toward The Melting Pot. I'd only taken a few steps before I froze. Jerking backward, my eye caught that of a hooded man staring at me from across the road. A blast of ice-cold shivers hit me with full force. He's back, and he's watching me? A hissing sound had the hairs on the back of my neck standing to attention. Where was Eli when I needed him?

A throaty growl purred to life in my ear and I bolted upright in my bed. I sucked in a lungful of air, my chest soaking it up like a lifeline, as if it were the last breath of air in the universe.

"What the...?" I blinked several times, letting my eyes adjust to the pitch-black darkness. A familiar growl sprung to life beside me. "Miss Saffron?"

"Of course." Miss Saffron purred deep in the back of her throat as she rubbed herself against my arm.

I brushed my teased bed hair from my face and let out a long sigh. "Well, that was an interesting dream, hey Missy? Come here," I said, picking up the fur ball in my arms, her coarse top coat scraping against my forearm. Her body tensed and my back stiffened. I snuggled her into my neck, stroking her soft undercoat in a bid to ease her anxiety.

"It's all good. It was just a dream." I reached over and flicked on my bedside lamp. "What time is it?"

"Four-thirty," said a petite female voice from the other side of the room.

"Ahhh." I dropped Miss Saffron and scooted up my bed, putting a sizeable distance between me and the unknown intruder. My pulse raced, and I squinted at the smallish figure half hidden behind the dresser. Miss Saffron stood on all fours in front of me, poised to attack. She snarled a low protective hiss toward the intruder. "Who the hell are you? And what are you doing in my bedroom at four-thirty in the morning?"

A hurt gasp echoed. "Really? Is that any way to greet an old friend?"

"Old friend?" I gripped my pillow to my chest. A lot of good the mass of feathers would do me if she attacked me. "Who are you?"

An excited bubble of energy bounded out and stood at the bottom of my bed, hands on her hips like a superhero here to save the world.

My jaw dropped. "Tr—Trixie?" I stuttered out against my dry throat. Surely, I was dreaming? I blinked half a dozen times and rubbed my eyes. Nope, she was still standing at the base of my bed. Her expression went from happy-go-lucky to annoyance in a split second.

I ran my hand up and down Miss Saffron's spine. "Easy girl. It's all right."

Trixie frowned and folded her arms across her sparkly pink blouse. "You know, you still snore. I thought you'd grow out of it when you got older. Guess not."

"I do not snore," I snapped. "Besides, you're not real. I'm dreaming. I must be having an episode if I'm hallucinating my imaginary childhood friend."

Realising the seemingly friendly interchange between us, Miss Saffron arched her back and circled herself, then snuggled down in a ball of fluff beside me.

"Oh really." Trixie's eyes narrowed and her lips pinched together as if she'd just eaten a sour lemon. She grabbed a cushion from the end of my bed and pitched it at me with full force. I squinted and turned my face to the side, my hands shooting up like a jack-in-the-box blocking the projectile before it landed smack in my face.

"Aw, what did you do that for?" I asked. My gaze caught Miss Saffron, who had burrowed herself under the warm quilt. I shook my head and glared daggers at her static body. "Lot of help you are."

She lifted her head, turned her golden oval eyes on me and purred. "I think you can handle this one by yourself, Evelyn." Actually, it was more like a grouchy smirk. "You're a big girl, you can take care of yourself."

"Where did the cat come from?" Trixie asked as she flopped down on the end of my bed. "You never had one when I visited last time."

"Feline," Miss Saffron murmured against her paw. "Cat is such a common term."

I glanced down at Miss Saffron and a warm glow filled my chest. As quickly as it arrived, it faded into a tight ball of tension that sat heavy on my heart. "After my parents died."

Trixie gulped the lump in her throat and her face fell. A cloud of gloom filled her expression. "Oh yeah, I remember. I'm so sorry. I wanted to visit, but I just didn't know the right words to say. Then you moved in with your aunt and time kind of got away from me. And then it seemed inappropriate to bring their deaths up after such a long time."

My heart shattered each time I remembered Aunt Edie breaking the news of my parents' death. "Aunt Edie took me in after they died, and it was then I found out I was a witch, and that probably explains why I can see you now. They keep telling me my powers are increasing all the time. Miss Saffron is my familiar. She arrived not long after I moved to Saltwater Cove. She's a kind of protector of sorts. Although she wasn't very intuitive this morning. She obviously missed your entrance."

"This might be an obvious question, but you're going to have to explain it to me." Trixie paused and jumped up onto her haunches. "Your cat is grey, most witch cats are black, and why is she called Miss Saffron when saffron is orange?"

I smiled at the memory and scratched behind her ear. A velvety sigh of appreciation hummed through her body.

"Not long after she arrived, she got into the spices in Aunt Edie's pantry, the saffron in particular. And Aunt Edie's pantry is a place you do not want to mess with. She had it all over her paws and mouth and she looked so cute. Somehow the name stuck."

Trixie smiled a half-hearted smile and pursed her lips.

"You're not a hallucination, because hallucinations don't throw pillows. I'm sure you didn't come back to talk about my cat."

"Feline," Miss Saffron said, her aggravated tone did not go unnoticed.

I glanced down at the grey ball of fluff and put my finger to my lips. "Shhh."

I smiled and reverted my gaze back to Trixie. My stomach knotted as she began twisting a clump of long blonde hair around and around in her fingers. A nervous action if I ever saw one.

"Well…funny you should ask. I kinda need your help," she said.

The pleading tone in her voice took me by surprise. "My help?"

She nodded and twisted faster and faster. "I'll come straight to the point. You see…I'm an elf. A real live elf from the North Pole."

My eyebrows shot up, and an estranged giggle filled my throat. "An elf? From the North Pole?"

"Yes, an elf." She pulled off her cute pom-pom topped beanie and pointed to her Spock shaped pointy ears. "See? Why do people act so astounded when I tell them I'm an elf?" She replaced her beanie, clenched her hands into fists and shoved them in her lap. "Is it so hard to believe? I'm an elf and I work in the North Pole with Santa and Mrs Claus. Do I not look like an elf?"

Now I've seen everything. Who knew my childhood imaginary friend wasn't imaginary at all, but a real live elf?

"So why do you need my help?" I asked. The floodgates on her mouth and eyes opened simultaneously, and I sat in awe of her animated facial expressions.

"I'm at my wits end, but I know you can save me from a fate worse than death…banishment from Santa's Village. If I'm banished, I may as well be dead."

Banishment from Santa's Village? Is that even a thing?

She explained in detail how her life had turned from one disaster to another in the last twenty-four hours.

"I worked so hard this year and I was nominated for Elf of the Year and made the finals. My mum and dad were so proud. Anyway, there were six finalists, and I did it, I won. I beat them all. You have no idea what an honour it is to win. It means Santa has chosen me…*me* out of every elf in Santa's Village." She paused and placed her hand over her heart. "As his numero uno, his number one elf and with that comes major responsibility."

"Wow, I had no idea. Congratulations." I handed her the tissue box from beside my bed. "Why the tears?"

A fresh round began, and she hiccupped a few times before continuing. "One of *the* most important roles as Elf of the Year is to look after the list."

"The list?"

She huffed and rolled her eyes to the roof. "*The* list. The naughty and nice list. The one Santa takes to deliver the presents to all the children."

A sliver of sun fighting to rise behind the hills reflected off the glass window and caught my eye and I squinted. I squeezed my lips together muffling a yawn. "If you have such an important role, why are you in jeopardy of being banished?"

She wiped her damp cheeks leaving her skin all splotchy. "Because Muffins Buttersong, the runner-up, stole the list and I have to get it back before Santa knows it's missing."

"Why not just ask for it back?" It seemed a simple enough solution to me.

Trixie's eyes clouded over. "Because he's lying dead on a slab in your morgue."

My jaw dropped and my voice appeared to have gone walkabout. The tip of my nose tingled as it registered the cool morning air. I shivered and pulled the quilt up higher, warming my chest.

Trixie blew her nose and a high-pitched squeal pierced my eardrums.

"Santa cannot know I lost the list. If it gets out, I'll be banished from Santa's Village forever. My life may as well be over. You have to help me get it back. You just have to." Her voice almost hit hysterical decibel level and Miss Saffron burrowed herself farther under my quilt. I'm surprised it didn't wake Aunt Edie.

My heart tore in two as fresh tears watered her eyes. "Okay, calm down. Of course, I'll help you. That's what friends are for, right?"

Her expression turned from doom and gloom into a breath-taking smile in a nanosecond.

"I knew I could count on you."

"No problem," I said, pausing to let another yawn escape. "When the sun is fully up, we'll pop into the police station and ask for it back."

Her eyes widened, and she shook her head side to side in small jutting movements. She sprang off the bed and began pacing, all the while her hands shaking as if she were drying nail polish. "No, it will be too late. We have to get it now. If a non-magical person looks at it, it will disintegrate on the spot and it will be as if it never existed."

"Oh." That changed things a little.

"We have to go in and get it now," Trixie blurted.

I gasped at her presumption that I would break the law. "I am not breaking into the police station and stealing *the* list from a dead elf, even if it's…" I paused and glanced at the clock. "…five-fifteen in the morning."

The floodgates opened again, and she threw her arms up in the air and flopped face down on the bed sobbing uncontrollably. "I'm doomed," she said, muffled into my bed quilt.

I sighed and my core temperature began to rise. "If you want me to help you, you're going to have to quit the hysterical crying. I have an idea."

"You do?" she said, shooting off the bed and frantically wiping her eyes dry.

I folded my arms across my chest. "Yes, I do."

"Oh my God, thank you, thank you, thank you." She squealed and threw her arms around my neck squeezing the life out of me.

I tensed and my back stiffened under her emotional outburst, but it wasn't long before my heart melted, and I revelled in her warm embrace. I returned the hug.

"But no more crying, okay?"

Trixie bolted upright and placed her right hand across her heart and held her left one up with her pointer and index fingers crossed. "I give you my solemn elf promise I will not cry anymore. Unless of course we can't get the list and we fail, then all bets are off."

I giggled and rolled my eyes. Throwing the quilt off I startled Miss Saffron, and she arched and stretched. I gave her a quick scratch behind the ear and smiled at her soaking up the attention. "I'll expect you to hold the fort until I sort this out. Can you do that for me?"

A silky purr hummed against my fingers and she nodded. "Need you ask?"

I glanced over my shoulder as I headed for the bathroom. "Wait here while I get ready. Don't leave this room. Got it?"

"But…"

"Got it?" I repeated, sterner than the first time.

Trixie nodded. "Got it."

Beaming a smile at me, she jumped on the end of my bed, sitting crossed legged.

It's going to be a long day.

CHAPTER FOUR

"This is your plan?" Trixie asked. "Hiding behind the bushes beside the police station?"

I pulled my winter coat tighter around my chilled neck and watched as Detective Huxton pulled his black Suzuki Grand Vitara into the parking lot.

Trixie followed my gaze. "We've been waiting for the cute policeman to arrive?"

"Cute?" I said, baulking at the thought. I guess I never looked at him that way, though I couldn't say the same for Aunt Edie. I remember how she tried to hide her racing heart rate every time he was near. She wasn't fooling me for a second. The memory of Detective Huxton's proposal fresh in my mind.

There is only one woman who has had my love and will hold my heart in hers for as long as I live and that is you, Edith Peyton. I love you and I know you love me too. Then there is only one course of action forward from this moment.

Aunt Edie's eyebrows had raised, and all she managed to say was "Oh?"

Marry me and make me the happiest Leodian who ever walked the planet. I love you Edith Peyton and I want to spend the rest of my life with you. I want to show you every day how much I love you.

"Oh yeah. He's the bee's knees. I could fall into his sexy dreamy eyes and live there forever." Trixie's high-pitched voice dissolved the euphoric memory and brought me crashing back to the present. She flattened her hands over her heart and sighed a swooning sigh.

The heat oozing off Trixie warmed the nippy morning air. My stomach did a 360 at her dreamy, yearning, far off look. Please don't tell me that's what I look like when I'm looking at Tyler?

Note to self: never swoon over Tyler in public.

"Can we focus please?" I asked. She cleared her throat and stood upright. "That's better. This is how it's going to play out and I want you to follow my instructions to the letter. Understand?"

Trixie's back stiffened and she gave me a cheeky mock salute. "Yes, ma'am."

The corner of my lip threatened to turn up into a smile, so I bit the inside of my cheek. With a huff, I huffed and refocused my thoughts on the task at hand. "I know for a fact the visiting medical examiner is not arriving until a bit later in the morning. I want you to wait by the back delivery door. I'll go in first and excuse myself to go to the ladies. I'll let you in and you get the list and then get out of there as soon as you can."

"Can't you just do a spell to magically get us inside without going through all this drama?" Trixie asked.

"I wish. I'm still a graduate witch for one more year and the only transportation spell I know involves a potion." My shoulders slumped and inch or two. I won't be a graduate witch forever. Then look out world, here I come. "You're not the first person to remind me of that fact. If you weren't in such a hurry, I'd suggest we go back home and I'd make one."

I felt a delicate hand skim my shoulder, and I turned to see a warm smile radiate Trixie's expression. "This will work just as good, I'm sure. I have every faith in you. You've never let me down before."

Locking my frustration away, I nodded and stood. Squinting, I pointed toward the blue delivery door around the back of the police station.

"Once you're in you'll have about fifteen minutes tops. Clear?"

"Crystal," she said, with a nod.

I stood on the top step of the police station and through the glass I could see Detective Huxton busy at his desk. Knowing it was still an hour before official opening hours, I tapped on the glass door. Nothing, he didn't even lift his head.

"He must be really into whatever he's reading," I muttered. I slipped a woollen glove off and my fingertips tingled as the cool air hit them. I tapped again. This time, there was no way he would ignore the racket I made. His head shot up and he stared straight at me.

"About time." I threw him the biggest smile and waved him over.

He was quick to unlock the door, and I shot past him. My heart rate picked up as he frowned at me. Rubbing my hands together, I said, "Oh my gosh, thank you. I can't believe how chilly it is this morning. Can you?"

He relocked the door. "No chillier than yesterday or the day before for that matter. What can I do for you, Evelyn?"

Realising I posed no threat, he headed back to his desk, and I followed, jumping around like I had ants in my pants pretending I was colder than I was. No sooner had he sat down, he sprung up again as if he'd sat on a porcupine.

"Has something happened to Edith? Is she okay?"

"Whoa, calm down. She's fine," I said, taking the seat next to his desk. "But I am here to discuss something that concerns her and you for that matter."

"Oh?" His tone was suspicious. He sat and leaned back in his chair, his wariness extending his standard police pose.

"Your wedding date," I said, gifting him a huge smile contradictory to my insides, which housed a tumultuous storm brewing. "As you know, it's been quite a few months now since you proposed, and you haven't set a date or even talked about an engagement party. I was thinking it would be a great idea if we gave her a surprise party. What do you think?"

He sat frozen a moment, almost statue like. Was he even breathing? He blinked a few times and finally found his voice. He raised his eyebrows. "I'm not sure that's a good idea. Edith has been very clear that she didn't want to rush into anything, and I respect her wishes."

I nodded. "I know, but I expect that's just nerves talking. I bet deep down she wants to celebrate your engagement with the rest of the town. She probably is just waiting for you to make the first move." I paused and channelled some of Harriet's superb acting skills. I pressed my hand to my belly and groaned.

"Aw, darn it."

"What's wrong?" His brows creased, forming a dubious glare.

"This stupid cold weather is playing havoc with my bladder." I stood and shuffled from foot to foot. "Do you mind if I use the ladies? I swear I'll be quick and then we can get back to discussing my surprise engagement party idea for Aunt Edie."

He nodded toward the back corridor. "No problem. I'll still be here when you come back."

"You're a life saver. Thank you." I grinned, turned, and moved double time. Turning the corner, I bypassed several non-descript doors finally pausing at the ladies' door around the next bend. I pushed it open for effect and then hurried past, straight to the delivery door.

My pulse raced. I turned the lock and opened it to find Trixie doing jumping jacks a few metres away.

"Trixie," I whispered. She continued with her make-shift exercise routine. My chest tightened, and I called out slightly louder. "Trixie."

She jerked to a dead stop and spun, her jaw dropping in a moment of startlement. Regrouping, she hurried inside.

"Sorry, my bad," she whispered. "It was freezing out there. Give me the weather at the North Pole any day."

The storm in my stomach resurfaced. I pointed to the door that read 'Morgue' in big black bold letters.

"You'll find the body through that door. I have no idea where it will be, you'll just have to search until you find it." She nodded. "Like I said, you'll have about fifteen minutes. I don't want to outstay my welcome otherwise he might become suspicious and I'm sure Wade is to arrive in the not-too-distant future. If you finish sooner, go out to the front door, and discreetly wave through the glass doors and I'll see you. Got it?"

She nodded and took off toward the morgue and I headed back to the ladies. A flash of heat whooshed through me as I pushed the door open. Pulling my gloves off, I shoved them in my pocket and flushed a toilet before heading to the wash basin. Splashing cold water on my face I leaned against the edge and stared at my strained reflection in the mirror.

"Why do you do this to yourself? Because you have a soft spot for those in need and you know it."

I glanced at my watch and sighed. "Great, he probably thinks I've fallen down the toilet by now." Heading back out, I sucked in calming breaths with each step. The warmth of the internal heating hit my face as I entered the main area. My nervous insides began to thaw along with my extremities.

Everything is going to work out just fine...Everything is going to work out just fine...Everything is going to work out just fine.

Plonking myself back down in my chair next to his desk, I covertly shuffled and repositioned myself to get a clear view of the front door. I let out a long sigh of relief.

"That was a close call. That will teach me to have two coffees before I leave home."

He grimaced and kept reading the paper in front of him. "Are you sure you've never seen our John Doe around Saltwater Cove before finding his body yesterday afternoon?"

I stiffened and shook my head. "No, sorry. Like I said yesterday, he's not one of the elves working with us at Santa's Photo Booth, or in the Christmas display. Maybe he was just visiting for the concert."

"Hopefully we'll know more after Irene gets through with the autopsy," he muttered.

Please be done soon, Trixie.

"Back to Aunt Edie," I said, cheerily. "Have you given any more thought to my idea of a surprise engagement party?"

He placed his pen down and swivelled in his chair to look at me. His Mediterranean green eyes sparkled at me, gluing my backside to the seat. I swear he was reading my mind. God, I hope not. Can Leodian's do that?

"Why a surprise party? Is that something your aunt would like?" he asked, very non-descript, almost like he was questioning a suspect.

"Who doesn't love surprises? Or parties? Granted the last big one we had at The Melting Pot Café, Prudence turned up dead, but I swear that was the first time that has ever happened." My gaze caught a familiar pink fluffy beanie sailing through the air on the other side of the front door and my stomach knotted. There it goes again. That's one way to grab my attention. I smiled and put my gloves back on. "Well, I've taken up enough of your time. I know how busy you are, especially in the silly season. Just think about it okay. I want to do something special for the both of you and your engagement should be celebrated with family and friends. Just promise me you'll think about it?"

He nodded and stood up. "Sure. I'll walk you out." Always the protector. At least I know Aunt Edie's safe when he's around.

"You're too kind," I said with a playful giggle. I exhaled as a sharp click behind me confirmed he'd relocked the door. By the time I'd made it back to Trixie, my stomach knots had doubled. Seeing her ashen white face and moist eyes tripled them.

Ice-cold smoke blew from my mouth as I spoke. "Let's get inside the car so I can crank up the heater." She followed and promptly burst into tears as soon as I slammed my door shut. I fussed around in the glovebox and found a new pack of tissues. Handing it over, I promptly reminded her. "You promised no more tears."

Her head shot up, and she pulled a tissue from the packet and blew her nose. Then blew it again. And again. My eardrums took one hell of a beating. How can someone so petite make such an explosive racket when they blow their nose? I'd hate to hear her sneeze.

"I also said all bets were off if we failed to get the list back and guess what?"

My breath seized in the back of my throat as a fresh bout of tears broke.

She continued, "There was no list to be found anywhere on his person *and* it gets worse."

"Worse? How could it possibly get worse?"

She nodded and sniffed. "Not only was there no list, I'm pretty sure someone is trying to frame me for his murder."

My jaw dropped. "Are you serious? How can you be so sure?"

"Because I found *this* beside his body." She reached into her pocket and pulled out her fist scrunched tight. She opened her palm flat to reveal a silky pink cord. "It's my dressing gown belt. Someone used it to strangle Butters. As Elf of the Year, I can enlist the help of the runner-up to help me with my new duties and that includes information about the list. Sort of like the runner-up in Miss World Pageant can help the winner if she is unable to fulfil her tasks. I'm guessing whoever did this, killed him for the list or because they thought he had the list or knew where it was."

The blood drained from my face. "You stole evidence?"

"I...yes...no...I...um," she said, fragmented. Trixie pressed her hand against her breastbone and wilted back in the seat. "I didn't know what else to do. It was beside his body and it has my elf DNA all over it. You have to help me. You have to come back to Santa's Village and help me find the real murderer and the list. Although, the missing list won't mean much if I'm facing elf prison for murder."

My mind raced searching for a plausible reason to stay in Saltwater Cove. *Tyler.* We're supposed to finish our Christmas shopping together this afternoon. "What? I can't go to Santa's Village. I have commitments here."

"Yes, you can," she blurted, an octave higher. "Anyone can visit Santa's Village if they are accompanied by an elf. If you help me out of this mess, I promise I'll return this cord into evidence. It has to be one of the four remaining finalists. I'm almost convinced of it. I can't do it alone. We prove one of them killed Butters, find the list and Christmas will be saved. All the children will get their presents and we'll avoid a cataclysmic disaster of the teary kind. Just think what heroes we'll be if we save Christmas?"

Cataclysmic disaster of the teary kind? Oh my goodness, Harriet's vision of crying children. This is what it meant.

Great. Why does the happiness of children all over the world have to fall on my shoulders?

A shudder swept through my body as if I were standing under an icy cold waterfall. Trixie's bottom lip quivered, and I squeezed my eyes shut.

"Okay, I'll help you. Between Harriet, Jordi, Tyler and myself we should be able to knock this over in no time and be back by dinner time." My belly dropped like a cement brick as soon as the words left my lips.

"No, no, no," Trixie said, shaking her head vehemently. "I can't rock up at Santa's Village with four adults in tow. They'll know something is up for sure. It has to be just you."

My forehead tightened. "Me? I can't do this by myself."

"Yes, you can. I know you can. You have me to help you and I have someone who can help us when we get back to Santa's Village. Please."

I glanced at her pleading eyes and I was a goner. "Okay…fine."

A brimming smile spread across Trixie's face and she grabbed my hands in hers and squeezed until they turned white. "Thank you. I don't know how I'll ever repay you."

"With Christmas in two days, I'm sure I can think of a few ways to return the favour." I kicked over the engine and took off back home. "But how about for now we keep my unexpected visit to Santa's Village between you and me. I'm sure the last thing Santa needs is an invasion of paranormal beings from Saltwater Cove."

"Agreed."

CHAPTER FIVE

Turning down our street, I noticed Harriet's car already in the driveway. Damn! That woman is an eager beaver when it comes to perfecting her cooking techniques. It wasn't enough to win *Witch Wonder-Best Baker* at the last Saltwater Cove Annual Show, she wants to make sure she can defend her title with something even better.

"Let me handle Aunt Edie and Harriet," I said, pulling in behind Harriet's car. "Just follow my lead. As far as they know you're an old friend visiting."

She muffled a snort. "Your aunt's a witch, right?" I nodded. "Then what makes you think she won't see straight through your lie?"

"It's not a lie, well, not all of it," I said, locking the car and ignoring the few drops of rain that started falling. "You are an old friend and you are visiting, so no lie. More like a slight bend of the truth. You used to visit me before I came to live with her so she shouldn't suspect a thing if you follow my lead."

"Works for me." Trixie halted half way up the steps and grabbed my forearm, her nails clawing through my winter coat. "What in the name of all things Christmas is that divine smell?"

I bit my bottom lip as I peeled her fingers away one by one. I drew in a deep breath. The spicy scent of gingerbread filled my nostrils and my stomach grumbled. "That would be Harriet's cooking. She's making gingerbread houses under Aunt Edie's expert tutelage."

"Santa Claus, can we taste some pleeeeeeeeeeease?" she said, begging, her chestnut brown eyes twinkling like glittering snowflakes.

I shook my head. "How about we focus on clearing your name and finding the list first? Then you can have all the gingerbread you want."

She nodded and grinned like a Cheshire cat. "Okay, but I'm not likely to forget a promise that involves yummy food."

"Follow me." I rolled my shoulders back, thrusting my chest out. Here goes. Turning the door handle I flounced into the kitchen, Trixie close behind. "Morning everyone. Those gingerbread houses smell heavenly, Harriet," I said, in my best happy-go-lucky tone.

"Evelyn darling, what are you doing out so early?" Aunt Edie paused and her eyes narrowed zeroing in on the additional person in the room.

Harriet turned, mixing bowl in one hand and a spatula covered in gingerbread batter in her mouth. Her brow creased.

"Evelyn?" she managed to mutter around the object in her mouth.

Aunt Edie grabbed a towel and wiped her damp hands. "I had no idea you'd already left this morning. When Harriet arrived, she mentioned you must have put your car in the garage last night. I insisted Harriet not disturb you, so we started on the gingerbread houses for the Christmas orders. She's such an eager-bever when it comes to cooking. Who is your friend, dear?"

I planted my feet and dumped my bag on the kitchen table between a bowl of liquorice all-sorts, white marshmallow snow and jars of candy canes. I kept my focus strong and committed to getting Trixie out of here before a gazillion questions rolled in.

"This is an old friend of mine, Trixie. She was in the neighbourhood and thought she would stop by for a visit. She called just as I was heading to bed last night and we decided to catch up for an early breakfast. You know how beautiful our sunrises are and she's only here for the day. I wanted her to appreciate every inch of our beautiful town."

Aunt Edie pursed her lips in thought and her face tightened.

Trixie piped up. "It was amazing, so beautiful. You must be Evelyn's Aunt Edie," Trixie said outstretching her hand. "She's told me so much about you."

Aunt Edie shook her hand and tilted her head. "In one morning? I guess you struggled to get a word in then."

My eyes widened, and I looked at Trixie, praying she could get us out of this one. Trixie grinned and her words shot out of her mouth like a locomotor on high speed. "You got that right. She raved about her life in Saltwater Cove and if it wasn't for you taking her in after her parents died, she would have surely given up on life."

"Really?" Aunt Edie said, crossing her arms.

Trixie nodded. "She told me how amazing it is to live and work with you every day in The Melting Pot and how you helped her come to terms with being a witch."

I did? I don't remember telling her that much about Aunt Edie. In fact, I don't remember telling her anything at all. It appears there may be something to this naughty and nice concept after all. If elves know everything about you, I expect Santa does as well.

"It's true," Harriet said, wiping the gooey mixture off her lips. "You're not only helping Evelyn, you're helping me as well, and not just with teaching me how to be an award-winning cook, but also helping me become an official member of your coven."

Aunt Edie's gaze shifted from Trixie to me to Harriet and back again. She smiled. "I better not let all this praise go to my head then." The tension milling in my chest began to dissolve.

"We're going to head off again on another sight-seeing expedition before The Melting Pot opens and I have to get to work."

I wasn't born yesterday, young lady. If I'm not mistaken, you're hiding something.

Trust Aunt Edie to pick up on my nervous anxieties. I wish I had more warning before she popped into my head.

It's all good, Trixie needs my help with something, that's all.

She frowned. *Should I be worried? Are you in some kind of trouble?*

No, of course not. I made a promise to Trixie and keeping my promise is important. You taught me that. You will be the first witch I call on if I find myself out of my depth. Promise. I'm asking you to trust me for now. Please?

Evelyn, over this past year you've been in some pretty hair-raising situations. I worry about you, that's all.

I know, but you don't have to. I'll be fine. After all, it's Christmas in a few days and I'll not let anything spoil the day for us.

Okay, but you will explain all this to me when you can.

A moment of understanding passed between us and I nodded.

"If you two are done chatting, do you think you could let us all in on the conversation?" Harriet huffed and crossed her arms. She pursed her lips and swapped her gaze from Aunt Edie to me, then back again. "You forget, not all of us can communicate telepathically. That's something that runs in your family, remember?"

A warm light-hearted laugh escaped Aunt Edie's lips. "My apologies. Sometimes I get caught up in the moment. I was just asking, Evelyn if everything was okay and if she needed my help."

I smiled and shook my head. "And I reassured her everything was fine."

Harriet asked in her usual bubbly tone. "If you want to spend more time with Trixie, I can cover your morning shift if you like." She placed a tray of gingerbread walls in the oven.

I'll need you to do more than cover my shift at The Melting Pot.

Butterflies swarmed my belly. "You're a gem. That would be wonderful. I was about to show Trixie the inside of The Melting Pot before it opened. Do you want to come with us?"

Harriet nodded; her eyes glistened like crystals in the sun. "Sure."

"Great." I grabbed her hand and dragged her through the adjoining door to Aunt Edie's witch themed café. Trixie skipped behind us, then she paused by the door and turned back. "It was lovely to meet you."

Aunt Edie gave a brisk nod. "Likewise."

Once the door closed behind us, I spun Harriet around and grabbed both her hands in mine, adrenaline racing through my body. A niggle in the base of my neck warned of an impending headache heading my way. I hated keeping Aunt Edie in the dark, but there wasn't time to get into it now.

Harriet's jaw dropped, and it was the first time she registered not all was as it seemed. "You didn't come in to show Trixie the café, did you?"

Trixie and I shook our heads in unison.

"No," I said. "But I do need your help." A monotone purr echoed from the counter behind Harriet. Miss Saffron stood to attention, her tail standing straight up in the air like a ruler and the fur on her back spiking. "Yes, yours too, Miss Saffron." She nodded her understanding. Gosh, I love this cat. She may get into her fair share of mischief but she's always there for me when it counts.

Harriet's eyes widened. "Anything. Besides, I kind of owe you for everything you've done for me over the past year or so. You know, saving my life, letting me come to work at The Melting Pot with you.

Not letting me go to jail for a murder I didn't commit."

"Harriet." I paused and squeezed her hands. "You're my best friend, I'd go to the ends of the earth to protect you. Now, without going into too much detail, I need you to cover for me maybe more than just this morning, but I promise to be back as soon as I can."

"Back? Where are you going? Are you in any kind of trouble?" Harriet asked, concern edged her words.

Trixie butted in. "Evelyn's not, but I am." Her animated expression changed from one emotion to another in a nanosecond as she spoke without taking a breath. "In a nutshell, I'm an elf and I live and work in Santa's Village. I won Elf of the Year and I'm in charge of Santa's delivery list and it was stolen. The body you found in the park is Butters Muffinsong, the runner-up elf who I suspect stole the list. Someone murdered him with my dressing gown belt and now Evelyn is coming back to Santa's Village to help find the list, catch a murderer and save Christmas."

Harriet stared at Trixie, a slight frown marring her expression. I cleared my throat and pointed to Trixie. "What she said. Can you cover for me? I promise I'll be back as soon as I can."

"Of course. Is there anything I can do?" Harriet asked. "I may not have as many witch skills as you but surely there's more I can do."

"Yes, and this is really important. Aunt Edie already suspects something is up, so whatever you do, don't let it slip out. If she finds out, she'll feel obligated to tell Detective Huxton and goodness knows what will happen next. We have this two-way street thing where we're supposed to keep each other in the loop, I tell him what I know and vice versa. But this time I know I can sort it without his help. I just need a little time." I blurted, my chest tightening at the thought.

Harriet's eyes glazed over as though she were heading into another vision and then her gaze diverted to Trixie. "I get it now."

"What do you get?" Trixie and I said in perfect unison.

"This all has to do with my vision, the one I had about all the crying children." She paled and looked straight at me, my heart seizing in my chest. "You have to save them, Evelyn. You have to save all the children from a Christmas without presents."

I nodded. "I will, I promise, but I need your help to hold the fort down here and keep things as normal as possible. Apart from being an awesome witch, you're the best actress I know and if anyone can keep a secret, it's you."

A beaming smile spread across Harriet's face and she nodded. "Hell yes, I am. You can count on it. Now get out of here so you can save Christmas."

CHAPTER SIX

Trixie said the portal to Santa's Village was under Swallows Bridge, the old stone bridge at the end of Dead Man's Hallow. Harriet, Jordi, Tyler, and I used to hang out on the banks of the river by the bridge after school. I can't say I've ever seen a portal anywhere near the bridge, but then again, I've never really looked. I couldn't deny the mysterious atmosphere surrounding the ancient structure. Lately, whenever I passed Dead Man's Hallow, my insides electrified.

We walked along the esplanade heading toward Dead Man's Hallow, my head pounding like a jackhammer with each step. What started off as a niggle in the back of my neck was now a full-blown torrent of pain thrashing inside my head. As if I'd just gone ten rounds with the heavyweight champion of the world.

I should have taken some Aspirin before I left The Melting Pot.

I pressed hard on my temples and squinted. Trixie stopped a few metres ahead of me and I almost barrelled right over her.

"Hey, I may be smaller than you but no need to remind me." Her body stiffened. "Come on Evelyn, what is with you? Can't you walk any faster? The clock is ticking on my life."

She huffed and resumed walking and I picked up the pace to keep in step.

"Sorry," I said, rubbing my forehead. "I'm battling a major headache I hadn't planned for." That'll teach me to keep secrets from Aunt Edie.

Trixie didn't stop the hectic pace. "That's a bummer. Don't you have a spell you can do to get rid of it? After all, you are a graduate witch and I'm sure you know a healing spell. What good is being a witch if you can't use your powers to help yourself in a time of need?"

Her words hit me like a snowball right in the face. I stopped dead in my tracks and stared at her as if she were speaking gibberish.

"Why do I never think of using my magic when it's a simple fix?" It was a rhetorical question, but Trixie shrugged anyway. "I suppose it comes from spending the first half of my life with my parents void of magic."

The prospect of being pain free sent a bubble of excitement dancing up my spine. I held one hand to my temple and the other open an inch off the other and said, "Pain and suffering come to rest, leave my body at my request. With this spell please disappear, pain be gone, and all is clear."

My fingertips tingled and a thawing sensation worked its way down my fingers to my palms. A bluish-green twisting beam of light circled my head and a transient flash of white scattered dots passed before my eyes and then they were gone, along with my headache. My eyelids flew open, and I filled my lungs with a delightful fragrance of salty air mixed with the scent of the floral flowers lining the esplanade. Intoxicated in a moment of calm, I almost forgot where I was headed.

"Better?" Trixie asked, her lips thinned as she waited for recognition.

"Much better." I nodded and smiled. "I've been reminded of late that the full extent of my powers is not yet known. They're developing all the time. Lucky me, I guess." We resumed our trek toward Dead Man's Hallow walking side by side. "Before we get to Santa's Village, how about you fill me in on the elves you believe may have had something to do with the stolen list and Butters' murder. The abridged version."

"I'm not 100% sure. I think I'm 95% sure at least, maybe 98%. Then again I could be—"

"Trixie," I snapped, breaking her continual line of chatter. "If you don't get to the point soon, we'll get to Santa's Village and I'll be none the wiser."

She flushed and a cute crimson blush circle appeared in the centres of her cheeks.

"Oops, sorry. I guess my brain sometimes moves faster than my mouth. An occupational hazard working in Santa's Village. We have to be thinking ten steps ahead all the time otherwise we would never make our Christmas delivery deadline." She cleared her throat and her eyebrows rose. "Working for Santa is the most rewarding job, but every elf knows if they are crowned Elf of the Year it can open up a whole new world of opportunities. There are always six finalists. I won, Butters Muffinsong, rest his soul, was the runner-up leaving four remaining elves."

"And you think one of them stole the list and killed Butters?" I asked, my chest tightened under the constant hectic pace.

"I do." She nodded, fully convinced she was speaking the truth. "The competition is fierce. In the past, I've known elves to do whatever it takes to win. Winter Mistleball took out sixth place. She's nice enough. If I'm honest, I don't know how she made the finals. Talk about clumsy. Jealousy reared its ugly head when she found out I scored top marks and, according to her, she barely passed. She's secretive and I know she is hiding something behind that pretty smile of hers."

We turned the corner, and I puffed a sigh of exhaustion as the old stone span bridge came into view at the end of the road. "Who came in fifth?"

"Ginger Cuddlecane. She works in dispatch and runs a tight ship. The 'no-nonsense-don't-mess-with-me-or-I'll-make-you-regret-it' kind."

"What makes you say that?" I asked, following Trixie onto the grass path. A familiar squelch under foot squeaked with each step. Last night's snowfall had melted away leaving a soggy wet grassed pathway to the bridge.

"Because she told me," Trixie snapped, her eyes rolling skyward. "This was her first year in the Elf of the Year competition and she made it to number five which is a solid effort. She was very clear. I should keep out of her way. Fourth place belongs to Pinecone Hustlecheer. He's a nice enough guy and out of all of them he is the last one I would suspect, but he did lie to me so now I'm not so sure. And finally, Fuzzle Bustlemitton. This is his third year in the finals, but he never seems to be able to crack the top spot. He's what you would call a 'yes man,' always ready to please Santa and Mrs Claus. Some call it a yes man, I call it a suck up."

Trixie stopped at the top of the steps leading down to the water's edge and I pulled up just in time to avoid another collision. My heart raced while beads of sweat hung above my brow. It's the middle of winter, for goodness' sake, and I'm sweating like it's summer.

I looked at Trixie and she stood frozen as a statue with a fixed look staring down the staircase.

I placed my hand on her shoulder and she turned. A broad smile spread across her face.

She smiled. "Just in case I forget to say it later. Thank you."

"You're welcome," I said, giving her shoulder a squeeze. "Now don't you think it's about time we saved Christmas?"

She rolled her shoulders back. "And not a moment too soon."

"Lead the way." Trixie took off, and I followed, my stomach rolling in a continual somersault as I got closer to the ice-cold water.

Please tell me I don't have to go swimming to reach the portal.

We reached the opening of the first stone archway and I peered in. The green moss-covered interior resembled the floor of an enchanted forest. Beautiful and serene. The recent winter rains had filled the dams and the water ran in a continuous stream through the arches. The gushing sound was music to my ears.

Trixie grabbed my hand and pulled me toward the centre of the archway.

"You're not going to throw fairy dust on me like Tinkerbell, are you?" I asked.

"Oh, you're so funny, Evelyn," Trixie sniggered. "Besides, she's a fairy, I'm an elf. It wouldn't work, anyway. I'd need elf dust, but that would really only help you fly and nowhere near strong enough for where we're going."

"Oh…so, what's the plan?"

Trixie stopped and turned. "You remember when I used to visit when you were younger and we'd sing Rudolph the Red-Nosed Reindeer?"

I nodded, not exactly sure where she was going with her question.

She continued. "Rudolf had one particular game he used to like to play, do you remember what it was?"

"Sure," I shrugged. She clenched my hand and a zing shot up my arm as we said in unison. "Marco Polo."

A blinding light exploded all around me and I held my eyes shut, my breath seizing in the back of my throat against the force of weightlessness floating my body above the ground. My mind spun for all of five seconds and then…thump. My feet hit the ground with a thud. A cascade of shudders vibrated from my feet up to the top of my head.

"We're here."

Already? That was the shortest trip through a portal ever. Since I've never been through one before, I guess that's as long as it takes.

"You can open your eyes now, Evelyn."

The energy in Trixie's voice spurred me on and I slowly peeled my eyelids open. I gasped and my jaw dropped. I couldn't decide where to look first. My body buzzed with a newfound adrenaline. It was everything I imagined Santa's Village to look like, and more. Much, much more.

I blinked my eyelids several times, positive I was dreaming. Nope, it's still here. "Is this for real?"

"Sure is." Trixie sucked in a deep breath and smiled. "Home sweet home. As Dorothy would say, and we all know there's no place like home."

I stood utterly dumbfounded at the beauty before me. It put our Christmas display in the church hall to shame. "It's like a proper village and all."

"Of course, it is. What did you expect?" she asked, sighing heavily.

I shrugged and shook my head. "I don't know, but not this. That's for sure. It's…it's the most amazing, stunningly beautiful place I've ever seen."

We stood between two gigantic pine trees covered in snow and fairy lights that opened the gateway to Santa's Village. Buildings and houses of all colours, shapes and sizes lined the streets. Most were built with wooden logs and all were expertly adorned with Christmas themed decorations. Snow covered every surface, and it sparkled like diamonds. My gaze wandered up to the huge mansion high on the hill at the other end of the main street. It was lit up like a high energy firecracker for the whole town to see.

"I'll give you one guess who lives up there," Trixie said.

I tapped my finger against my cheek. "Mmm...if I was to guess, I'd say the main man himself...Santa, and Mrs Claus." Trixie smiled, pleased with my guess. "I want to see all there is to see, but for now we have to focus on the reason we're here."

"Right." Trixie pulled her beanie down over her pointy ears. "First step is to get past the town guard. Pfft, piece of cake for the Elf of the Year."

A high pitched screech reverberated in my ears like nails down a chalk board.

"Aw, what was that?" A massive force collided with the centre of my back pitching my whole body forward face first into a pile of fresh snow. It was as if a baby elephant was sitting on top of my torso, crushing my lungs from the outside in.

Trixie's voice rung out. "What the...Harriet?"

CHAPTER SEVEN

"Surprise," Harriet muttered, half-heartedly.

Every part of me registered the cool effects of lying face down on a blanket of snow. While it wasn't overly cold, it was wet, and I didn't fancy walking around all day in wet clothes. It's not like I can call into my local clothing boutique and buy a new outfit in my size.

"Harriet, will you get off me?" I said, through a mouthful of soft icy snow. The sudden release of pressure off my chest was a welcomed relief.

Harriet righted herself, jumping up on her feet. She reached down and offered me a hand up. I accepted, not one to ignore a gift horse in the mouth.

"Oh gosh, I'm so sorry, Evelyn. I guess I haven't mastered the landing yet. I'm sure yours was way more elegant than mine. I've never used a portal before. In fact, I never knew they existed. Pretty neat, huh?"

"What are you doing here?" I asked, brushing specks of sparkled snow from my clothes. "How did you get here? If you're here, who is holding the fort back home helping Aunt Edie prepare for Christmas?"

She rocked restlessly on her feet the whole time, her gaze shooting between me and Trixie.

"I know, please don't get mad. Eli is covering for me. I had a tough time convincing him that you weren't in danger but in the end, I didn't give him much of a say."

"Eli? Who's Eli?" Trixie asked with an inquisitive expression.

"My Guardian."

Her jaw dropped into a perfect O. "Your Guardian? Why do you need a Guardian?"

I rubbed my forehead and sucked in a deep breath. "It's a long story and one I'll be happy to share with you when we clear your name." I turned back to Harriet. "Care to explain why you followed us?"

"After you and Trixie left, I had a vision. It was the same one I had yesterday when we found the body...of the screaming children, except this time it was amplified ten times. It was a warning, and I just couldn't stand by and do nothing."

"What does it mean?" Trixie asked, her expression grim.

"I'm not sure, but it must be important otherwise why did I see it twice?" Harriet took her gloves and beanie off and shoved them in her coat pocket. "Have either of you noticed even though there is snow everywhere, it's not actually cold?"

Trixie giggled. "Of course, silly, it's the North Pole. It snows all year round, but it never gets too cold."

I closed my eyes for a moment and took a deep breath. "Harriet…what do you think your vision means?"

"Well, I'm almost positive it's linked to Trixie's lost list and if you don't succeed in finding it, children all around the world are going to be broken-hearted when Santa arrives with no presents."

Trixie paled and tears welled in her eyes. "We fail?"

"No." The word burst from my lips before my mind kicked into action. "No, we cannot fail. Harriet sees a vision of the future, but it's only one possible future. It can change if we want it too."

"Oh, thank goodness," Trixie said, her hand pressed to her chest.

Harriet's gaze finally spotted Santa's Village, and she stood stock still. Her mouth gaped and her eyes drank in the beautiful sight.

"Wow…just…wow. I knew it would be amazing, but I never imagined it would be this stunning."

I followed Harriet's gaze and paused a moment, joining her in adoration.

"It really is something, isn't it?" She silently nodded.

"You still haven't told me how you got here?" I asked.

"Once I realised what my vision meant, I followed you and Trixie. I tried calling out, but it was no use. You were engrossed in your conversation. I caught up with you just as you said your final words and disappeared. I have to admit it took me a few goes to find the right place to stand, but…" She paused, holding her arms open and grinned. "Tada, here I am."

A gruff hoarse voice yelled out of nowhere. "Who goes there? Speak now intruder or ye shall forever pay the price."

The intense, powerful voice kicked my pulse into triple time and my heart skipped a beat. I spun to see an elf marching toward us all territorial like. His bright red sash, police hat and boots screamed, 'don't mess with me, or else.'

Trixie held her palm to her mouth and whispered behind it, "Let me handle this."

Fine by me.

Harriet and I took a casual step back as Trixie stepped in front of us. "Rusty, why do you insist on greeting people who visit our home in such a grumpy way? Anyone would think you're Grumpy dwarf from Snow White."

I squeezed my lips together, muffling an escaping giggle. He resembled Grumpy in a cute elf way.

He threw his hands up in the air and sighed in resignation. His tone softened. "Trixie, what are you doing bringing strangers to Santa's Village? This is our busiest time of the year or has that piece of information slipped your mind?"

Trixie stood her ground, feet planted and her hands on her hips and stared at him. "Am I not Elf of the Year?" She paused and waited. They stood opposite each other in an awkward silent stalemate. "And as Elf of the Year, I am entitled to additional privileges only I am privy to, am I not?"

She paused and waited again. A slight questioning frown marred his expression and Trixie stuck her chin out and her back stiffened in triumph. "I don't have time to go into detail now, but I'd like to introduce you to my friends, Evelyn and Harriet."

Harriet plastered a wide grin on and stuck her hand out. "Pleased to meet you, Rusty. Santa's Village is so lucky to have a strong handsome elf protecting it from the evils of the world. I mean with someone like you at the helm, with those big muscly shoulders and all, Santa's Village is sure to be safe."

Here we go again, Harriet and her superb acting skills at play. This woman never ceases to amaze me.

A cheeky grin turned the corner of his lip up and if I didn't know better, I'd say he was blushing. He smiled and his facial expression softened. Way to go, Harriet. A niggle bubbled inside my belly and I jumped on the acting band wagon.

"I have to agree with Harriet. Santa's Village could not be in better hands. I'm Evelyn and it's my pleasure to meet such a strong robust elf. It gives me peace of mind knowing our good friend, Trixie, is being looked after by someone of your calibre."

"Aw, shucks," he muttered, kicking the loose snow around with his boot. "That's real nice of you to say. Any friends of the Elf of the Year are friends of mine."

He stepped aside, and we walked past. He called after us.

"If you need any help at all, you know where to find me."

All three of us threw him a huge smile and kept walking at a quickened pace.

"Thank goodness that's over. This way," Trixie said, leading us round a back alley away from the busy main street. "You do realise he's going to want to know all about you both now?"

"I'm sure he's harmless," Harriet said.

Her crafty grin had me smirking on the inside. "I'm sure he takes his work extremely serious, and that makes him the best elf for the job."

Trixie's pace didn't flounder. We trekked down a few streets and turned up another lone alleyway. If we were in Saltwater Cove, I'd be worried about the unknown danger, but what could happen in Santa's Village?

"We're going to need some more inside help and there's only one person I trust as much as you ladies and that's my best friend, Hope Hollybow," Trixie muttered, more to herself than anyone else. "She's helped me out of a scrape or two in my time." Trixie huffed, shook her head, and stopped mid-stride in the middle of the alleyway. "Oh no, I don't believe it. This is all we need." Trixie winced, and her anguish infused words clawed at my gut.

"What's wrong?" I asked around the lump in my throat. I followed her gaze to the woman heading our way.

"Juniper Jollycheer, that's what or should I say who?"

"Who is Juniper Jollycheer?" Harriet asked, pulling up beside Trixie. "If the name is anything to go by, she sounds like a lot of fun."

"Try the total opposite," Trixie groaned. "If she is fun, then she's hiding it deep inside…deep, deep, inside locked away from everyone. I don't think I've ever seen her shed an ounce of fun in my entire life. A grumpy know-it-all is more like it. She prides herself on being the town gossip. If you want to find out anything, ask Juniper, she's guaranteed to know and if she doesn't, give her half an hour and she'll find out for you."

A sour taste rolled around in my mouth. "She can't be that bad."

Trixie's eyebrows raised, and she tilted her head up to look at me. "Have you ever seen the Christmas movie Home Alone 3?"

Both Harriet and I nodded. "Have you?" I asked.

"Of course. Santa requires all elves to see every Christmas movie ever made to ensure his legacy is kept intact. Some have come close, but so far, so good. Anyway, remember the character Mrs Hess, the grumpy nosy neighbour?"

My insides squirmed just at the thought of the woman.

Harriet sighed and pursed her lips. "That bad, huh?"

"Worse. A gazillion times worse. But unlike the movie where Mrs Hess turns out to be nice, Juniper hasn't a nice bone in her body. We don't have any more time to waste and to go back the way we came would just take more time. Just follow my lead." She resumed her trek.

It took less than a few minutes before we were within metres of Juniper Jollycheer. I may be in another land and my mind may be running overtime, but she sure looked like she was dancing in the street to me. An odd thing for the town grouch to be doing.

I glanced at Harriet and she shrugged and tilted her head as if to say, 'beats me.'

"On the mith day of Ristmas, Santa have to me…"

"Good morning, Juniper, I hope you're having a lovely day," Trixie said, in a sweet non-confrontational tone.

The woman abruptly stopped singing and glared at me and Harriet. Her eyes narrowed, and she sized us up and down. I held my breath, anticipating an outburst of some sort. Her gaze dropped to Trixie and her arms shot open and a huge grin spread across her face.

"Blixie Blowbell." She threw her arms around Trixie and I saw Trixie visibly stiffening under Juniper's grip. She shook Trixie from side to side in one of the biggest hugs I'd ever seen. "Blixie…Blixie…Blixie, you darling child. Did you know it's only twoo days until the spost important day of the wear?"

A drunk grumpy elf singing Christmas carols and dancing in the street. This is a first for me.

Trixie pulled back doing her best to escape the loving onslaught of the woman and her heavy sherry-laden breath. "Yes, I did know, Juniper. It appears you decided to start celebrating a little early this year."

Juniper burst out laughing and put her finger to her puckered lips. A fresh sparkle in her golden-brown eyes.

"Shh, don't tell anypune, will you? The Knitting Knights finished a bummer baby knit twis year a day early so Ivy brought out the runch."

"Don't you mean punch?"

She swayed unsteadily on her feet. "That's what I said, runch."

Trixie wangled her way out of the woman's grip and side-stepped her swaying body. "Congratulations. I must be off now. Elf of the Year duties are calling."

Before Trixie could escape, Juniper leaned over and pinched her rosy-red cheeks. "You reserve every success, dear Blixie. Ren Santa read your name out I jumpered for joy. I'm so glad Winger Cuddlemaine didn't win. She's a bit of a pushy nosy busy-body if you ask me." Juniper looked right then left then right again and leaned in closer. She whispered, "Wanna know a secret?"

A secret?

We huddled in a tight circle. I raised a questioning eyebrow at Trixie and she nodded. Juniper opened her mouth to speak and her sherry-laden breath hit me in the face. It was like being buried under ten pounds of candy. "Don't tell anyone but I was out attending to my poinsettias and I saw Gwinger and Butters Mittonsong sneaking out of Santa's workshop yesterday morning. They looked real susp…ssup…ssss…"

Trixie rolled her eyes. "Suspect?"

"That's it…suspect," Juniper said, followed by a string of hiccups. "They were snaking off…" Hiccup. "…somewhere I'm sure of it." Hic, hic. "…*And* she doesn't like my Christmas cookies. She says they're like eating rocks." Hic. "The nerve of that woman. My tistmas rookies are the best in the village."

Trixie rolled her eyes and beckoned us to follow. "Thanks for the insight, Juniper. Bye."

I did my best to keep the giggles in, but one glance over my shoulder at the dancing singing woman and a riot of laughter burst free. "I'm sorry. She just cracks me up."

"Me too, but at least we got a lead to follow," Harriet said, wiping a tear from her eye.

"We sure did. I wonder why they were sneaking out together? Let's hope Ginger will be forthcoming with the answer. Juniper probably won't remember she told us, anyway." Trixie walked up a cobbled stone path to the back door of a small log cabin. "I bet she wakes up tomorrow with no memory of the interchange and one whopping hangover. She doesn't normally drink alcohol at all, even at Christmas time. She probably didn't even know Ivy had put it in the punch."

"More luck for us." Trixie pushed the wooden back door and stepped inside holding it open. I stopped inside and my nostrils were assaulted with the mouth-watering scent of cinnamon and nutmeg. I licked my lips and my stomach grumbled its displeasure with being ignored. "What are you cooking?"

"Nothing, my house always smells like cinnamon and nutmeg. It's an elf thing. You should smell it when I am cooking," she said, with a sly grin.

"You're on." My gaze instantly soaked up the homely wooden interior expertly decorated in all things wood and Christmas. "Wow, this place is stunning. You sure know how to make a house feel like a home."

An exquisite stone fireplace took pride of place at the end of the main living area accentuated with two impressive stacks of wood piles lined up on either side. Two honey brown antique looking leather couches filled the main living area and with its comfort inviting me in, I was drawn to them like a bee to a flower. The warm yellow lights glowing off the wooden interior walls sent a loving rush of emotion into my heart.

"Trixie, this is the cutest place," Harriet said, swirling around. "I love the wooden winding staircase. What's at the top?"

"My bedroom." Trixie locked the door, stripped her coat off and hung it on the coat rack inside the door. "Make yourselves at home. I'll call Holly."

"Evelyn, I want a house like this in Saltwater Cove. It's perfect, don't you think?" Harriet said, moving to check out the dining area. "And I can pretend it's Christmas all year round."

I placed my coat on the hook next to Trixie's and headed for the longer of the two couches. It flirted with me, tempting me to give in to its delicious ways. I ran my hand over the smooth soft leather, and it moved like silk under my touch. When I eased myself down, I savoured every inch of it as it engulfed my body into a lovable hug. I closed my eyes and breathed in its rich luxurious scent and my head swooned.

"As long as you have one of these couches, you can have any house you like."

Trixie stood at the end of the couch and cleared her throat. "Comfy?"

My head rested on the head rest and in a moment of pure relaxation, I sighed and let go of all the built-up tension I'd stockpiled since yesterday afternoon. I opened one eye and squinted at Trixie.

The jingle jangle of the doorbell interrupted the calm atmosphere, and I sat up eyeing Trixie. "Is that Hope?"

Trixie nodded and headed for the door, wringing her hands at her waist. Harriet joined me on the couch, softly humming the tune of Jingle Bells. Moments after Trixie opened the door, a chattering whirlwind blew in holding a glass bowl filled with delicious trifle. She stopped dead in front of the couch, her voice silenced at the sight of Harriet and me.

"Um, Trixie, isn't that your friend, Evelyn, you told me about?" she asked, in a strained tone. "The same friend you used to visit when she was younger?"

"Yes. I know what you're going to say, and I can explain."

Hope spun and glared at Trixie, her voice lowering to a whisper. "Explain? Why in the name of ginger nut cookies would you bring a witch to Santa's Village?"

CHAPTER EIGHT

"Two witches," Harriet said, holding up two fingers.

Hope's jaw dropped and the pitch of her voice shot through the roof. "Two witches?" She raced over and placed the trifle on the kitchen bench. "You brought two witches? One is bad enough, but two? Trixie, what were you thinking?"

Trixie's hands were wringing together so fast I feared she'd twist them right off. My heart broke for her. "Hello Hope, I'm Evelyn and this is my best friend, Harriet. We are witches, good witches that is. We're here to help Trixie and believe me, we do not want to cause you any distress."

She harrumphed and folded her arms across her chest. "Too late for that."

Trixie raced over and grabbed Hope's hand, dragging her to the other couch. They both sat and Trixie sucked in a deep breath before diving into an explanation. "Hope, you're my best friend in the whole entire universe and I would never do anything to put you in danger. You have to believe me. Evelyn and Harriet are here to help me get out of a bind that could see me stripped of the title as Elf of the Year and banished from Santa's Village forever."

Hope gasped, and her eyes widened. "No."

Trixie nodded and bit her bottom lip. "Yes, I'll explain everything, but I'm going to need your help to clear my name." An awkward silence fell over the room and Hope's eyes narrowed, darting from Trixie to Harriet then landing permanently on me.

"Trixie," I said, fixing my gaze on our hostess. "I think you better start from the beginning and don't leave any detail out."

Trixie nodded and swallowed. "It all started when *the* list was stolen."

"You lost the list?"

The horror in Hope's voice elevated my pulse tenfold.

"I didn't lose it, it was stolen. At least I think it was. In fact, I'm pretty sure it was. I thought it was Butters Muffinsong who stole it, but I was wrong."

"Where is the list now?" Hope asked.

"We don't know, that's one of the reasons we're here," I said, in a soothing calm tone.

"That and the screaming children," Harriet said. "Who are going to be heartbroken if they don't get their presents this year."

I continued. "Trixie has a pretty good idea who did it and we're here to help her get to the bottom of it."

"What's the other reason?"

"To prove I didn't murder Butters," Trixie said, her posture faulted as she spoke the 'M' word.

Hope shot off the couch like a firecracker and her voice screeched. "Butters is dead? You murdered him?"

"For goodness' sake, I did not kill Butters." Trixie pinched the bridge of her nose. "But someone did, and they used the belt of my dressing gown to frame me. How long have you known me, Hope?" Trixie paused and raised an eyebrow. "All our lives, right?"

Hope nodded and sank back down on the couch. Trixie continued, focusing solely on Hope. "And in all that time have you ever known me to kill or hurt anyone, even a bug, let alone another elf?"

"No, I'm sorry." Hope's chin lowered, and she ran a hand through her strawberry red hair. "I guess it was a shock. It's a lot to take in all at once. The missing list, a murder and two witches."

Harriet chimed in. "That's why we need your help. Children everywhere are going to be hurting if we don't find answers. I suggest we keep this between the four of us. We don't want a village-wide panic to ensue. We have no idea what the murderer might do if the cat is let out of the bag."

"Agreed. I have to deliver the list to Santa by the end of tonight and I'm running out of time. You know he likes to do a final check before he starts the delivery and that can take a while."

Hope nodded. "So, you think whoever stole the list, murdered Butters?"

"Yes and dumped his body in Saltwater Cove where Evelyn and Harriet live. Somehow they must have worked out my connection to Evelyn." Trixie reached over and squeezed Hope's shaking hand. "Will you help me?"

Hope's eyes watered and her soft smile suddenly lit her face up. "Of course. I'll help you. Whatever you need. I never really thought you murdered anyone."

Hope and Trixie hugged it out and the tension in the room evaporated. A comfortable ease fell between the four of us. "Trixie has narrowed the suspects down to the four remaining contestants that she beat out in the Elf of the Year competition. The time of death was four-twenty yesterday afternoon."

Hope frowned and my stomach dropped. "What is it?" I asked. "Do you know something that could help us out?"

She shrugged and repeatedly ran her palms down her thighs. "Maybe…maybe not. You say Butters was murdered at four-twenty yesterday?"

There were nods all round. "Yes."

"Then I'm pretty sure it can't be Pinecone Hustlecheer. I saw him out my office window down by Mistletree Pond. As I work on the top floor of the toy factory, and I can pretty much see a one-eighty of the outside through my office window and Pinecone was there all right, at that time. I remember because I looked at my clock on the wall and it struck me odd that he was taking an early break at four-fifteen instead of his normal time of five."

How can Pinecone be in two places at once? Here and dumping Butters body in Saltwater Cove. He can't.

"Pinecone simply would not have enough time to be in two places at once," I said, tapping my chin. This new information rolled around in my head like the wheels of a clock. "That may eliminate him as a murder suspect, but he still could have something to do with stealing the list. We'll still need to question him."

Hope's hand shot up in the air like a rocket. "I'll do it." She squealed and just about leaped off the couch. "We used to be pretty good friends in elf school, and I bet I can get him to open up to me."

"Perfect." Trixie stood, bounding with a newfound energy. "You speak to Pinecone and

Evelyn, Harriet and I will head over and talk to Ginger."

I followed Trixie through the enormous toy factory barn door and was instantly hit with the metallic scent of tinsel combined with sweet gingerbread. It had my stomach grumbling, demanding to be fed. It smelled just like the gingerbread house Harriet was making with Aunt Edie.

I gawked in awe at the hive of activity covering every corner of the factory. Elves built, sang, cleaned, wrapped, packaged, tied, walked, skipped, and even danced. Hypnotised by the flawless routine, I didn't know where to look first.

"Oh my God. This has to be *the* best toy factory ever," Harriet blurted, ripping the words right out of my mind. "How cool is this place?"

"It's the best place to work, that is, when my life isn't on the line." Trixie grumbled. "Ginger works over in dispatch. This way, it's the last stop before the presents get loaded into Santa's sleigh."

We followed Trixie toward the back end of the factory passing an oversized clock on the wall. An elegant calligraphy sign above it read, *Countdown until Santa's Christmas Eve Departure.*

"I guess no one is going to miss the deadline with a clock that enormous." I dodged fast-tracking elves on a mission. It appeared being a guest of the Elf of the Year had its perks.

We stopped by a counter underneath a platform housing boxes and boxes of already wrapped presents.

"That's Ginger Cuddlecane," Trixie said, pointing to a stocky elf dishing out orders like a well-oiled machine. She was a distinguished elf with dead straight midnight black hair pulled into a low ponytail at the base of her neck. With her black glasses and white lab coat, she had a preppy scientist look about her. Fingers crossed she's not the mad scientist type. Totally not what I expected.

Approach with caution.

"Hi Ginger. I hope this is not a bad time," Trixie said, in an over-the-top cheerful voice. "These are my friends and I was explaining to them how the factory works and how important your dispatch job was to the whole system and they insisted on coming to meet you."

Ginger stopped fussing with the papers on her desk and huffed. She grimaced and glared our way as if Trixie had told her she'd cancelled Christmas.

"What? Can't you see I'm busy?"

My pulse quickened and words blurted from my mouth in a continuous stream before I could vet them.

"You have no idea how excited we are to meet you, Ginger. Trixie's been raving about you and how you have one of the most important jobs in the entire factory ensuring the presents get out on time. How do you deal with the pressure? I'm positively sure I would crumble in a heap on the ground."

"There's no time," Ginger said, as a soft shade of pink floated up from her neck and planted itself in her cheeks. The stern, controlling glint in her eye was now overtaken by a shimmering blush. "I suppose I have a couple minutes to chat as long as we don't take too long. We are on a tight schedule, remember?"

"Excuse me, but what do you think you're doing?"

I spun and stood eye to eye with an elf atop a forklift. The unnerving suspicious glare in his eye had my stomach in knots. He looked important, but then again, they all did.

"I'm not sure what you mean?"

He jutted his chin out and glanced at Harriet and I. "Trixie…Ginger, you know full well safety is paramount in the workshop, even down here in dispatch."

"We didn't mean anything by it," Harriet muttered, leaning into my side. "Trixie was just showing us where all the main action happens."

"No need to get your tights in a twist, Noel," Trixie said, moving to stand beside Ginger. "We're not going to be staying long."

His brow creased and his grouchy voice rose an octave. "As Santa's appointed safety officer, it is my job to ensure the accident target stays at zero."

Trixie's brow furrowed. "How did you even know we were here?"

He waved a hand toward a collection of stained-glass windows high on the second level. "That's my office up there and from there I can see everything and what I don't, the cameras do. Remember, that was one of the new additions Santa made to the main floor to keep injuries down." He shook his finger in our direction. "Not wearing a hard hat and fluorescent vest on the dispatch floor is a no-no. You don't want to end up like Butters Muffinsong, do you?"

A cold shiver inched up my spine and my mouth went dry. Word of Butters' murder can't have spread that fast? Was it a mistake to trust Hope?

"W—what are you talking about?" Trixie's nervous tone didn't go unnoticed.

"The Lego incident two years ago. An expertly wrapped box of Lego destined for a boy in Atlanta fell off the packing pallet right onto his noggin. He was one lucky elf, only a short stay in the infirmary." His eyes narrowed, sending his brows into a purposeful wrinkle. "What incident were you talking about?"

Trixie giggled and brushed a dismissive hand toward Noel. "The same. I was just seeing if you remembered it."

Ginger huffed, rubbing her forehead. "Look, while this is a very entertaining trip down memory lane, we're wasting precious time we don't have."

I couldn't agree more.

She glanced at her watch. "I'm due for my break so I'll take it now and we can go to the break room and chat there. That way Noel's tights will stay in pristine condition."

He grimaced and backed up the forklift. "Ha, very funny Ginger. I'm watching you."

"Fine by me. Watch all you like, you might learn something," Ginger said, stripping off her white lab coat and donning a pink and green cardigan. "You know my impeccable work record speaks for itself. See you in forty-five."

She flounced off, and we trundled along behind. Harriet leaned in and whispered, "Gee, I wouldn't want to get on the wrong side of Ginger. I bet she can hold her own, but could she be a pushed to murder?" I nodded in agreement and thought the exact same thing.

Harriet walked into the break room first. I collided into the back of her stationary body and we both nearly face planted on the black and pink chequered tiled floor.

"What did you stop for?" I asked, rubbing the stabbing pain at the end on my nose.

"Look," she said, her eyes wide and jaw gaping. "I'm in heaven. I've died and gone to food heaven. This is the best break room I've ever seen. It has everything you could possibly dream of eating."

My hand slipped from my nose as my gaze followed hers. I breathed in the mixed scent of cinnamon, candy, gingerbread and coffee and my head swooned. My knees weakened at the thought of all the delicious food adorning the benches. It certainly gave The Melting Pot a run for its money. I licked my lips and a testy grumble worked its way up from my belly.

Ginger handed each of us a plate, albeit a small elf-size plate and a tray and headed toward the dessert bench. "Santa believes it's important to be fuelled when working in the factory. Whatever you desire, it can be made. It gets the best work out of us when we focus on the job and not our empty stomachs. The best part is it's open 24/7. Help yourself."

By the time I'd gorged the dessert bar, the salad bar and had my fill of fresh prawns and downed two coffees, my stomach sighed a big gigantic thank you. I looked over at Harriet and I couldn't help but giggle at the eighth piece of Christmas pudding she was shovelling into her mouth.

"Now, how can I help you?" Ginger asked, dabbing the corners of her mouth with a serviette.

Trixie cleared her throat and threw me an 'I'll-handle-this' look. "I was telling Evelyn and Harriet how important your role is as Head of Dispatch. You are responsible for making sure all deliveries go into the right basket and head to the right home."

"I can't imagine how much pressure you're under to get it right," Harriet said. "If you get it wrong, there could be major consequences."

Ginger's eyes glowed and a ruby red hue flooded her face. "*I* do not get it wrong. I can't be held responsible for others who stuff up. Yesterday's blunder was hardly my fault and I'll not be made the scape goat."

Now we were getting somewhere. I probed delicately. "Of course not. You were probably the one who caught the problem, am I right?"

She pursed her lips and gave a curt nod. "Darn tootin I did. I was supposed to clock off at three-thirty. Thanks to some nincompoop over in printing, who somehow managed to print double address labels for all the children in Amsterdam, I ended staying until after dark to sort the mess out."

I looked at Trixie and my heart tore in two as the sliver of hope faded from her eyes. "How frustrating for you. Did you have any help?" My polite way of asking if she can provide an alibi.

Ginger nodded and demolished the last of her chocolate cherry cheesecake. "If I was staying, then so was the entire floor until the mess was sorted. By the time I worked out what had happened and corrected it, it was way past seven. It could have been a major disaster if not for me. Thankfully, I was able to sort the problem before having to tell Santa. It was a close one."

Trixie stood and gathered the empty dishes and placed them on the used counter. "I'm sorry you had to deal with such a mix-up this close to Christmas. We'll let you get back to work." She headed for the door, her chin lowered in thought.

Harriet shrugged and shook her head. I sat glued to my seat; a forgotten morsel of the puzzle niggled in the back of my mind. It was taunting me, just out of reach of my memory. I watched Ginger stand and repeat the cleaning process with her own plate and tray. What was I missing? I racked my brain going through everything I'd learned since arriving in Santa's Village and then it slapped me in the face. Juniper Jollycheer. I slyly tapped Harriet's arm to get her attention.

"What is it?" she whispered.

I mouthed. 'Juniper' The glint of recognition in Harriet's eye matched mine.

I cleared my throat. Time to test my acting skills. "By the way, Ginger, congratulations." Ginger paused mid-scrape of her bowl and frowned my way.

"For what?"

"Oh, come now, don't be shy," I said, joining her, my pretend excitement a little over the top. "You and Butters Muffinsong, of course. A little birdy told us you were dating. Being with the love of your life is so romantic. Congratulations. Our lips are sealed. Right, Harriet?"

"Right." Harriet grinned and made a zipper action with her lips then locked it with an imaginary key and threw it over her shoulder.

Ginger recoiled, her skin turning ashen white. Her complexion paler than the crisp white snow outside.

"What…how…who told you such baloney? It's simply not true. Not true I tell you."

I gasped and my hand flew to my breastbone. "Really? We heard you and Butters had a little secret rendezvous yesterday morning, so we assumed you were together. Did we get it wrong?"

"You most certainly did." She raised on her tippy toes and glanced at Trixie pacing by the door. She muttered under her breath, "If you must know, Butters wanted to throw Trixie a surprise party and he was trying to enlist my help. We are not romantically linked, just the thought nauseates me to the core."

I slapped my forehead. "Gosh, how positively silly of me. I'm sorry to have jumped to such a drastic conclusion. Please forgive me."

"Evelyn...Harriet," Trixie called from the doorway. "I think we've taken up enough of Ginger's time, besides there are still more people to meet and places to see."

I spun on my heel and caught the slight tilt of Trixie's head toward the door. She repeated the action, glancing toward the entrance a number of times. She's either having a really bad eye reaction and a twitch in her neck or she has spotted something or someone out the window.

"Coming." I grabbed Harriet's hand and pulled her toward the door, my stomach turning in somersaults. I glanced back over my shoulder. "Nice to meet you, Ginger, and I promise your secret's safe with me."

CHAPTER NINE

The snow squelched and squeaked underfoot as we headed back to Trixie's place. "That is good news. We can cross Ginger off the suspect list. She was at work the time of the murder dealing with what sounded like a major disaster."

"Yeah, but what about break time?" Trixie asked. "She could have taken some breaks. She's quick and to the point so if she did kill Butters, she wouldn't have wasted time in doing the deed."

"It's possible, but if I'm honest, it really didn't sound like she was able to get away. I'm not even sure she took a break, but we could ask around a bit more I guess, just to be on the safe side. According to Ginger, the only reason she and Butters were together yesterday was because he wanted to throw you a surprise party and wanted her help."

"What?" Trixie stopped. "He was throwing me a surprise party?"

I nodded and my chest tightened as tears pricked her eyes. "Sounds like he was a pretty cool elf. The best thing we can do to honour his memory is find the list and bring his murderer to justice."

She sniffed back her tears and stiffened her jaw. "You got that right. Thank you for being here and helping me."

Walking into Trixie's place, we were confronted with a chaotic upturned mess and a frantic Hope rushing around picking up scattered cushions and righting chairs. My chest seized and nausea welled in the base of my stomach. Someone had messed up Trixie's house, on purpose.

I'm guessing they were looking for the list.

"Goodness me, what on earth happened here?" Trixie asked, her eyes wide and her hand flat to her forehead as she scanned the messy room.

"Thank goodness you're back," Hope said, rushing over and throwing her arms around her best friend. "I came over to tell you my news, and I found the place like this, all messed up. Who would do such a thing?"

"I expect whoever is after the list," Harriet muttered, picking up turned over lamps and shutting open drawers in the kitchen. "They're obviously getting desperate to break in and ransack the place."

"Oh, they didn't break in. The door wasn't locked," Hope said, looking blankly at Harriet.

"What?" Harriet and I said in unison. Harriet paused by one of the open draws in the kitchen.

Hope continued, her words escaping with a slight tremble. "We've never had a need to lock our houses in Santa's Village. Santa always believed in trust. He said if you can't trust a fellow elf, who can you trust?" Hope's complexion faded until all that was visible was a pale pink tinge at the top of her cheekbones. "I'm worried about you, Trixie. You must lock your door until this nightmare is over."

Trixie nodded and opened her mouth to speak Harriet's intriguing tone cut her short.

"Evelyn, I think you need to see this," Harriet said, staring at the contents of an open draw.

"What is it?" I asked.

"No," Trixie blurted, bolting towards Harriet and slamming the draw shut. "It's nothing, no need for you to look in there."

Harriet pressed her hands to her hips and tilted her head. "A box with Evelyn's mother's name on it is hardly nothing."

Did I just hear right? A box with my mother's name on it...how is that possible?

An icy shiver raced up my spine, goose bumping my skin. It was the first time since arriving in the North Pole the cold air had invaded my body. "What are you talking about?"

"You were never supposed to know about it," Trixie said, blocking the draw with her body, her complexion dropping to an ashen white.

"Know about what?" The jittery edginess to my voice startled even me. My throat dried, and I swallowed against the furball forming. "Trixie, what shouldn't I know about?"

She held up her hands in a surrender position. "Okay, okay, but please don't hate me. She made me promise…promise that I'd keep it safe. She said if it fell into the wrong hands, it could mean the end of Christmases forever."

A gasp from Hope echoed behind us. "End of Christmas. Perish the thought."

I scratched at my temple and a gazillion thoughts ran through my mind. Heat invaded my cheeks. "Trixie, when did you meet my mother?"

She huffed and her shoulders slumped. "It was the last Christmas before they died. Your dad had taken you ten-pin bowling to celebrate the end of the school year. I swear I had no idea your mother was home. I popped in to leave you a dream catcher and she caught me as I was leaving."

"That was you? I thought it was from her. It's beautiful, and it still sits on my dresser."

Trixie nodded. "She caught me with my beanie off and there was no use trying to hide my ears. She knew exactly who I was before I could even explain.

Then she told me she was a witch and gave me this." She paused and took the small box out of the draw.

My breath hitched as my gaze fell to the box in her hands. "What is it?"

Trixie shrugged. "I have no idea. I've never opened it. Like I said, she told me the contents could never fall into the wrong hands. That's why I had to bring it back to the North Pole with me and promise to keep it away from you."

"Oops," Hope said. "I guess that didn't work as well as you'd hoped."

Trixie's words played on repeat in my mind.

The contents could never fall into the wrong hands...the contents could never fall into the wrong hands...the contents could never fall...

The blood ran cold in my veins and my head snapped up and I looked at Harriet. "My mother was adamant that Trixie keep this hidden from me, right?"

Harriet nodded and shrugged. "So?"

"Think, Harriet." Adrenaline pumped through my body. "What else has my mother been adamant about be kept from me?"

"Um..." Harriet shrugged again and grimaced.

Her bewildered expression had me smiling. "I guess all that sweet food has numbed your brain cells."

"Hey, no fair," she said, faking hurt. "It's not my fault it was all you can eat."

"Tell us, Evelyn." Hope twisted her fingers and fidgeted with the tassels on her pink scarf. "What else did your mother keep from you?"

I stood, and they stared at me as though I were about to tell them the divine secret to the universe. "Anything to do with the relics and the Sphere, or Salis Van Der Kolt."

"Whoa." Hope's eyes widened. "He sounds like that bad dude from *Harry Potter*. You know, the one with the funny nose and is always trying to kill Harry. What's his name again?"

"Voldemort?" Harriet said, her gaze squinting at Hope.

Hope snapped her fingers in agreement. "That's him."

Harry Potter? Are you for real?

"Since when do elves watch Harry Potter?" I asked, catching sight of Harriet's bemused smile.

Hope rolled her eyes and Trixie joined with an exasperating huff. "Since forever. It's Trixie's and my favourite series. I mean that Daniel Radcliffe is such a honey."

A slight giggle erupted from the base of my belly. "Now I've heard everything."

"Can we get back to the situation at hand, please?" Harriet asked around her clenched jaw.

Trixie nodded and a cute raspberry blush filled her cheeks. "Of course."

"Sorry." Holly squirmed where she stood. "You have my undivided attention."

"That's more like it." Harriet turned to face me square on. "Go ahead, Evelyn. Finish what you were going to say."

My gaze caught the small box in Trixie's hand. Gone was the jovial sensation, replaced by a slowly growing knot. I sucked in a deep breath and slowly released it.

"Over the past year certain information has come to light that has put a question over my parents' death. I now believe they were murdered." I ignored the increasing gasps and continued. "It's come to light that black magic, among other things, has returned to Saltwater Cove and may have contributed to their deaths. Everyone concerned with their deaths was sworn to secrecy by the High Council."

"Wow, this is better than any Harry Potter movie," Hope whispered.

"Shh," Trixie said, waving her hand to silence her best friend. "Please continue."

"Thanks to my continual digging, the High Council granted me the ability to delve into their death as long as no one helps me, and I find out the details by myself. Through my investigations, I discovered the Sphere. It's the one object that can control all worlds, both witch and human, and if it were to fall into the wrong hands, it could prove the end of life as we know it."

Trixie's gaze dropped to the box in her hand. "Like the end of all Christmases."

"Exactly," I said. A prickle of icy air whisked across the hairs on the back of my neck. "The High Council believe Salis Van Der Kolt has returned to find the Sphere, and so do I. He's tried to find it before and failed. He's as evil as they come. From what I know, there are four relics and when found, somehow guide you to the location of the Sphere. How exactly, I'm not sure yet, but my parents hid the four relics and I intend to find them and destroy the Sphere before Salis can get his hands on it."

Hope's brow creased. "Wow, that sure puts things into perspective."

"I'm guessing what's in that box has something to do with the Sphere. It may even be one of the relics. At least I'm hoping it is." I held my hand out towards Trixie. "May I have it, please?"

I saw Trixie's grip on the box tighten and my stomach clenched. Her gaze dropped to the box once more. "I'm not sure that's such a good idea. Your mother asked me to keep it away from you."

"I know, but she also hadn't planned on being killed for her efforts to protect me and destroy the

Sphere. My only way to save the world is to find the relics and destroy the Sphere and to do that I need to see what's in the box." Neither Trixie nor Hope moved, but the tension within the room was growing, playing havoc with my racing pulse.

"Or…" Harriet paused, folding her arms, waiting until both elves were focused on her. "You could wait until Salis himself pays you a visit here in Santa's Village and retrieves the box himself. Mind you I wouldn't want to be here when he comes."

"Oh hell no," Hope said, shaking her head in short sharp movements. "Having two witches here is bad enough. Give Evelyn the box, Trixie."

Trixie let out an exasperated sigh and placed the box on the dresser. "Fine, but I'll not give it to you. Your mother asked me not to, but I guess if you find it by yourself then I'm not really giving it to you, and I haven't broken my promise to your mother."

Trixie's words played on my heavy heart. Breaking a promise didn't sit well with me.

"That's fair," I said, walking steadily towards the box. Although it was a smallish box, the magnitude of its unknown contents was like a volcano ready to explode under the pressure.

I paused a moment and bit my bottom lip. Even though I hadn't come to the North Pole to be confronted with my past, if it has anything to do with my parents' death and the Sphere, I'll take it.

My fingers itched to find out what was in the box. Holding my breath, I pulled the lid off and glanced in. A prickle behind my eyes stung as I fought back tears.

Oh, Mum, I miss you so much. I can't believe you kept the handkerchief I gave you for Mother's Day all those years ago.

I raised the box to my face and sucked in a lungful of air, the scent of my mother seeping through my nostrils. My heart tore in two all over again.

"Come on, Evelyn, don't keep us hanging," Harriet said, her voice full of bounce. "We still have a stolen list to find and a murder to solve."

Harriet's voice crashed through the moment of nostalgia swamping me.

"Right." I wiped my damp eyes with the back of my hand and cleared my throat. Reaching in, I pulled out the neatly folded handkerchief and a round metal object dropped to the floor.

"I'll get it," Trixie said as she bent to retrieve it. She held it up for all to see. It was covered in some sort of ancient calligraphy, sort of like the Egyptian hieroglyphs. "Woah, this is the most beautiful gold medallion I have ever seen."

Harriet relieved Trixie of the object and flipped it over several times. Her brow creased, and her lips pursed. "Mmm, what do you suppose it means?"

I shook my head, and a compounded heaviness invaded my chest. "I don't know yet, but I'm pretty sure it is one of the four relics I'm not meant to find." When I held my hand out, Harriet dropped it in my palm.

The instant reaction of the medallion to my skin was like a set of nerve cells dancing to their own beat. The medallion moved and jumped around on my hand as though it had a life force of its own. I gasped and the other three stepped back unsure of when it would stop. It must have only been going a few seconds, but it felt like forever. The reaction fizzled out and all four of us leaned in, glancing at the medallion in my hand.

"It's you, you're the key, Evelyn," Harriet said, her voice tranquil and full of sincerity.

"What are you talking about?" I asked.

"Look," she said, pointing to the surface of the medallion.

The weird letters started moving around as if they were unjumbling. My jaw dropped and my breath stalled. "What...how is this happening?"

No one moved or barely breathed, everyone's eyes focused on the moving letters until they stopped.

"That is the coolest thing I've ever seen. What does it say now?" Trixie asked.

I leaned in read, "To change one's destiny you must first discover the hidden truth."

Harriet's lips parted and her eyes widened. "See, I told you so. It did nothing when Trixie or I held it. It reacted to you, you're the key to solving this whole Sphere mystery, Evelyn. Your parents must have had the same thing happen to them and that's why they were trying to destroy it and all the other relics before Salis got his hands on it. I'm guessing that's why they were murdered."

My body tensed, and my hand quivered. My parents gave their lives to protect the ones they loved and my job is no different. Protect the ones I love no matter the cost.

My mind raced with all this new information, but it didn't negate the task at hand. I wrapped the coin back in my mother's precious handkerchief, put it back in the box and replaced the lid. My heartbeat quickened at the thought of my beautiful parents leaving this world prematurely.

Hope placed her hand softly on my shoulder. "Evelyn, are you okay?"

I bit the inside of my cheek then nodded. "I will be once I find the relics, destroy the Sphere and avenge my parents' death."

"So, a normal day's work for you then?" Harriet said, breaking the tense air. "You can do that with your eyes shut. My suggestion, for what it's worth, is now you know it's one of the relics, we put it aside and solve our other dilemma of the missing list and the murder of Butters before I get another vision of screaming and crying children."

CHAPTER TEN

"**O**f course, you're right," I said, tucking the box back inside the draw for safe keeping. I turned to Harriet and grabbed her hand. "Please don't let me forget to take the box home when we leave."

"I promise," she said, squeezing my hand.

I turned to Hope and shook off the thoughts of Salis and the box and refocused on our reason for being in the North Pole.

"Weren't you saying something about some news you found out?"

Hope nodded and slapped her forehead. "Yes, that's right. I almost forgot about it what with the discovery of the medallion." She glanced at the clock on the wall. "Oh gee, I have to get to work soon, but I wanted to tell you what I know. I'll be quick. Let's sit," she said, making herself comfortable in the single armchair.

"We think we've managed to cross Ginger off from the murder suspect list, although she still may have stolen the list. She was dealing with a major disaster at the time of the murder. She may have taken some breaks, but my gut tells me she had nothing to do with it."

"Well…" Hope's face lit up and her eyes danced like polished gems. She shuffled to the edge of her seat and cleared her throat. "I found out something very interesting indeed."

Oh, do tell. This could be the break we need.

Anticipation hung in the air. It was like the anticipation you felt the split second before jumping out and yelling surprise to an unsuspecting birthday guest.

"I was right when I mentioned Pinecone couldn't have had anything to do with Butters' murder. I've confirmed he was indeed out by Mistletree Pond."

I swear she paused for dramatic effect.

"He was out by the pond working out how to propose to Eve Bustlemyrrh." Gasps and mutterings filled the room.

"No way…"

"…how sweet…"

"Propose?"

Hope continued taking a big breath. "He was out there the entire afternoon. I asked around and several elves saw him. When I asked him what he was doing out there he broke down and confessed he was in love with Eve and was trying to work out the most romantic way of proposing. He was just the cutest. He was so nervous and wanted to make it a special night Eve would never forget. I gave him a few pointers, but if I were to say, this Christmas, Eve Bustlemyrrh is going to be one very happy elf."

"I'm really happy for Eve and Pinecone but we've hit another dead end." Trixie's gaze bounced from one to the other. "Where do we go from here?"

Hope bounded up and headed for the door, throwing her bag over her shoulder. "I'm going to be late for work if I don't get a move on. Call me if you find out anything. I'll touch base as soon as I can, and I'll see if I can get away from work early."

"Bye, Hope, and thank you," I said, waving. The sombre drop in mood flattened the vibe of excitement I had as I'd left the toy factory. "I think moving forward we're going to need to split up so we can cover more ground sooner."

"That's a perfect idea, Evelyn," Harriet said, leaning forward and resting her elbows on her knees. "There's still Fuzzle and Winter to suss out. We can speak to Fuzzle and Trixie can take Winter, then meet back here and compare notes."

A renewed sparkle ignited Trixie and her expression softened. "Yes, that might work, but they're both on shift at the toy factory. After the incident with Noel and the hard hats, you're not going to be able to walk around as easily without me."

Harriet shot up from the couch and clicked her fingers as if a light bulb switched on inside her head. "I've got it. Evelyn can do a disguise spell. I'm sure she can make us look like elves, then we'll blend in."

A disguise spell? I haven't done one of those in years. Can I even remember the spell?

Trixie's eyes widened, and she clasped her hands together in her lap. "Can you do that?"

I pursed my lips and smiled, ignoring the tightness in my gut. "I can, but it's been a while. I might be a little rusty."

"Pfft," Harriet said, flippantly. "It's like baking a cake. Once you learn, you can never forget." She turned in Trixie's direction. "Do you have a community newspaper or journal in town?"

She nodded. "Yes, there's the *Santa's Source*. It reports on important news and happenings in the village. Why?"

"I am just full of ideas this afternoon." Harriet flicked her leg underneath her backside and got comfortable in Hope's vacated spot. "Once we're in disguise, we can pretend we're doing an article on Trixie for the *Santa's Source* about her role as Elf of the Year. We'll be able to ask as many questions as we need, all in the name of research."

"That's not a bad idea, Harriet." I can't believe I didn't think of it. Re-energised by her idea, I stood and paced the outskirts of the room. A renewed bubble of adrenaline coursed through my limbs. "Give me a minute while I remember the exact spell."

My feet moved on rote in a circle around the kitchen table. My brain focused on remembering the words to the disguise spell. "Okay, you can do this," I muttered under my breath.

In plain sight I abide…No that's not right. In plain sight…my appearance will be.

I paused a moment, closed my eyes, and refocused. All of a sudden, they were there; it was as if the words channelled themselves right into my soul. I spun and two sets of eager eyes were focused on me, waiting patiently. Both stood like animated statues. "Okay, I've got it. You might want to stand back a bit, Trixie. If I remember rightly, it gets a little hot." Trixie nodded and shuffled back toward the kitchen entrance. "Come over here Harriet and I'll change you first." I licked my lips, my mouth dry.

"Make me a cute elf, would you?" Harriet said, stopping in front of me, the glow in her eyes intensifying.

As if I wasn't nervous enough already, now I have to make her cute?

"Harriet, it's a disguise, not a fashion show. We're catching a murderer here." My stomach knotted and my throat filled with the regurgitated taste of prawns.

I swallowed hard and focused on the task ahead. "You're not here to pick up a date. Once it's done, we're going to have to make a move. My spells don't last long but it should be long enough to find the answers we need."

"Okay." Harriet pouted and stuck out her bottom lip. "I just thought if you have to give me a disguise, why not make it a cute one?"

"Just stand still." I placed a hand on her shoulder and held the other vertical inches from her heart. I swallowed hard and said with strong conviction.

"In plain sight you need to hide, with this spell please do abide. Your appearance will now be an elf for one and all to see."

I held my breath and my pulse raced as a multicoloured stream of sparkles swirled from my hands around Harriet's body interweaved with mine. My hand filled with warmth and soon intensified to a point of pain. I pulled my hands back and rubbed my palms together. The knots in my stomach hardened, and my hands flew to my face covering a blinding flash that blasted the room. A moment of tense silence and then a strange voice.

"How do I look?" Harriet asked in a squeaky chipmunk voice.

I opened my eyes to see an elf dressed in a stereotypical Christmas outfit. Green and red striped stockings, a green mini skirt trimmed with red fringing. A white blouse and a green and red fitted vest complete with red glitter heels with curly tips. Long black curly hair hung down her back, neatly tucked behind a set of pointy ears.

Pleased as punch with my efforts, I smiled. Definitely an outfit Harriet would have chosen for herself.

"You look perfect," Trixie said, clasping her hands together at her chest. "Now your turn, Evelyn."

"Okay, stand back." I brushed my sweaty palms down my thighs and sucked in a deep breath. My pulse was running its own marathon. I placed one hand on my sternum and held the other inches off my heart and repeated the spell.

"In plain sight I need to hide, with this spell please do abide. My appearance will now be an elf for one and all to see."

My fingertips tingled and a surge of heat bled down my fingers through my arms and lodged in my chest. A familiar stream of multicoloured sparkles swirled between my hands and around my body. My eyelids lowered and a burst of heat lasting a nanosecond burned through my body and then it was gone.

I feel the same? Did it work?

A shiver goose bumped my arms, and I peeled my eyelids open one by one to see Harriet and Trixie standing opposite me, eye to eye, jaws dropped.

"What's wrong?" My hand flew to my mouth, shocked at the sound of my own voice. I squeaked just like Harriet. "Oh my, I sound so nasal."

"You sound just like me," Harriet said, through a high-pitched giggle. "Not only do you sound like me, you look exactly like me. We're twins. Now we're really sisters."

"What?" I sounded like one of the seven dwarfs from Snow White, with a cold.

Trixie shrugged. "I suppose that makes sense since it is the same spell you used on both of you. As long as it keeps your cover and lasts long enough for you to speak to Fuzzle, then that's all we need."

I knew Trixie was right, but an odd sensation stirred my insides knowing Harriet looked exactly like me. I shook the cobwebs from my mind.

"Okay, let's go over the plan one more time."

Trixie nodded and rolled her shoulders back. "While I speak to Winter, you and Harriet will speak to Fuzzle. You'll find him on the sleigh floor in the factory. He works in the packing department. He makes sure Santa's present sacks are filled with the correct number of presents according to the destination. Winter's lucky enough to look after Santa's reindeer, so I'll be able to find her in the stables. We meet back here as soon as we're finished."

The jingle jangle of Trixie's doorbell scared the bejesus out of me. "Are you expecting anyone?"

She shook her head. "No. Maybe it's Hope returning." She trotted over to the door and opened it just as it jingled once more.

CHAPTER ELEVEN

N ow that I know Santa's Village is all real, my entire body went into fan girl meltdown. The picture-perfect woman from my childhood Christmas stories dressed in a red velour tracksuit stood metres from me holding a pair of crumpled red velvet pants. My jaw dropped, and I had to physically push it up again.

Mrs Claus? I can't believe the *Mrs Claus is standing at Trixie's door. She's just as I imagined. Sweet and stunningly beautiful, although younger. I must ask her what moisturiser she uses. I got to get me some of that.*

"Mrs Claus, this is an unexpected surprise," Trixie said, in a heightened voice. "You've just caught me. I was about to head out."

Mrs Claus' eyes widened. She shook her head and her soft blonde-white ringlets bounced around her shoulders. She marched straight past Trixie to the middle of the room. Her voice quivered on the verge of tears.

"No, no, no, no you can't be going out now. I need your help. Santa needs your help. You're the only one I can rely on in a time of crisis."

Crisis…What crisis? And how can Trixie help?

Harriet and I looked at each other and we watched on as Mrs Claus practically had a full-blown meltdown in front of us. I always imagined her to be level-headed in a crisis. She was the one who kept Santa on his toes and in line. I guess everyone has a bad day or two.

Trixie's eyebrows pulled together, and a brand-new worry crease sprang to life. "Oh my gosh. Come sit and explain everything to me."

She sighed and flopped down on the couch, my couch. I could tell the soft leather soothed her just as it did me.

Her gaze swung around the room catching Harriet and me in the corner of her eye. Her back stiffened and her body went rigid. "You didn't tell me you had company."

"These guys? Pfft," Trixie slashed her hand nonchalantly to the side. "These are my friends. Evelyn and Harriet, meet Mrs Claus." She nodded politely almost like royalty. When it comes to Christmas, there *is* no one more royal than Santa and Mrs Claus.

"They're more like part of the furniture than company. You'll have to excuse the mess, we were doing a bit of redecorating. But they were about to go out to the back garden to pick some flowers, weren't you ladies?" Trixie's eyebrows shot up and the implications of her words were not lost on me. "I'll come and join you when Mrs Claus and I finish our chat."

My pulse raced. This was one of those moments that called for a split-second decision. I couldn't pass up the opportunity to meet my idol. I raced around the couch as quickly as my little elf legs would take me and clasped Mrs Claus hand. "It's an honour to meet you, Mrs Claus. I've always dreamed of this moment, of meeting you and here you are."

"Here I am," she said, a strained smile spread across her face.

"You're even more perfect in real life." My hand continued to shake hers, sending tingles up my arm. The uncomfortable expression on her face had alarm bells ringing in my ears. I dropped her hand and smiled.

I turned and caught Trixie's eyebrows raised and her head gesturing towards the back door. "Yes, that's right, just on our way out the door to pick flowers," I said, cringing at my new raspy voice. Nudging Harriet toward the back door, I turned and glanced over my shoulder. "Nice to meet you, Mrs Claus." I waved goodbye and pushed Harriet through the wooden door, pulling it closed behind me, all but an inch gap. I crouched down and pressed my ear to the door and heard the faint voices of Mrs Claus and

Trixie. My entire body buzzed with an adrenaline rush. I pushed my ear to the open gap, straining to decipher the conversation inside.

Harriet spun hastily and stumbled over her pointy shoes. Her mouth fell open. She whispered, "What are you doing?"

"Shhh," I whispered, hushing Harriet with my hand before beckoning her closer.

"Something is up with Mrs Claus and for all we know it could have something to do with Butters or the list. Either way, it could be vital information we need moving forward."

Harriet nodded and edged her way in pressing her own ear to the gap above mine.

"Like I said, you have to help me, Trixie. If Santa finds out, he'll never forgive me." Mrs Claus sobbed openly.

"I doubt that's possible. He loves you so much. Santa is a very forgiving man. Besides, it's not as bad as you think," said Trixie. "Actually, Mrs Claus, it's a real easy fix."

"Do you think so?" she asked. "I warned him about trying Keto, but he insisted on seeing it through to Christmas Eve and the pounds have been dropping off him. I'm so happy he's eating much healthier now, and he wanted to ensure he had extra room for cookies and milk this year. You know how he hates to disappoint the children. You know I'm not a seamstress and he wants these pants taken in by afternoon tea."

"Leave them with me, Mrs Claus, I'd be happy to adjust them for you. As Elf of the Year, it is my duty to help out anyway I can, even sewing. I'm your elf."

"Really? Thank you, Trixie. I knew I could count on you. If it weren't for you, I don't know what I'd do," Mrs Claus said, in a thankful tone.

"You've mastered cooking, so how about in the New Year we put sewing lessons on the list instead?"

"I like the way you think." There were giggles all round and then a solid click of the front door closing.

Trixie taught Mrs Claus how to cook? No way.

I pushed the wooden door open and followed Harriet back inside. Trixie sat holding up Santa's large pants with a frown on her brow, her lower lip stuck between her teeth.

"You taught Mrs Claus how to cook?"

Trixie paled and sat paralysed, Santa's pants hanging in the air, her eyes glued to mine.

"What? I thought you were out picking flowers."

"We were outside, listening through a crack in the door. You really didn't expect us to actually pick flowers, did you?"

She folded the pants and shoved them out of sight underneath an embroidered cushion. "I guess not. You have to promise you won't breathe a word of what you saw or heard to anyone, here or in Saltwater Cove. Mrs Claus may not be perfect like all the children's stories make her out to be, but she is the most amazing woman and mother-figure most elves will ever know. So, she may not be able to sew, but now she can cook like a champion. Forget she was even here, please?"

She clutched her hands tight in front of her chest and her eyes glistened over. It was enough to pull at my heartstrings.

"Trixie, it's okay. We would never do anything of the sort, and you have our word what we heard and saw never happened, right Harriet?"

"Right." Harriet threw her arms around Trixie and squeezed. "You're the best. Mrs Claus is lucky to have you. I hope when this is all over you will come back and see Evelyn and me in Saltwater Cove. Minus the drama and dead body."

Trixie returned the hug and pulled back, her gaze shooting between the both of us.

"Of course, but we have bigger candy to crush first. Now that I have to fix Santa's pants, I can't go to the factory with you and you can't waste the time waiting for me. You'll have to go without me."

"No problem. Evelyn can take Fuzzle and I'll chat to Winter," Harriet said, secretly pulling Santa's pants out from behind the cushion. Trixie's lips thinned and she crossed her arms as if to say, 'What are you doing?'

"Sorry, I had to touch them once. They're Santa's pants...*the* Santa." Harriet closed her eyes and rubbed the soft crushed velvet against her cheek. She cleared her throat and handed them back to Trixie. "Right, you take care of these. Come on Evelyn, we have a toy factory to visit."

"Wait." Trixie said. Racing to the top draw in her kitchen, she pulled out two notepads and pencils and handed them over. "You'll need these."

"What for?" Harriet asked.

She grinned. "If your reporter's doing a story on me, you better at least look the part."

The big oak barn door of the toy factory loomed ahead. A maze of answers was sure to greet us when we entered. The urgency of Trixie's situation hung over my head like a thunderous black storm cloud. Our schedule put back by our run in with a certain medallion. The growing knot in my gut was a clear indicator of Trixie's looming fate. If we don't find the list and the murderer soon, she'll end up banished for a crime she didn't commit. It wasn't enough to question the remaining two elves, we needed to push them all and force the culprit's hand into making a mistake.

My pulse raced as I grabbed Harriet's arm and dragged her to the side of the entrance, the crisp air biting my rosy cheeks.

"Aw, Evelyn." Harriet squealed, jerking her arm free as we hid behind a tall expertly decorated Christmas tree out of sight of the entrance. "What's the big idea?"

"Time is running out. We need to step it up. Just questioning them may not get us anywhere and we can't be certain it's going to find us the list or Butters' murderer."

"What did you have in mind?" Harriet asked, frowning, rubbing the spot on her arm my hand crushed as I dragged her from the pathway.

"I have an idea," I said. My mind raced a hundred miles an hour trying to fit the pieces together. "Someone still desperately wants the list otherwise why search Trixie's house? We need to draw the culprit out and the only way to do that is to make it known Trixie still has the list. We set it up so they think she is going to do one more check of the list later this afternoon say, three o'clock before delivering it to Santa. And we cross our fingers and hope it will push them over the edge."

Harriet stood still a moment and a multitude of expressions crossed her face. "Are we really going to put Trixie's life in danger?"

I shook my head. The thought sickened me to my soul. "Of course not, but we need to make it appear as such. You and I will be in hiding, waiting for them to arrive and once Trixie gets a confession out of them, we'll pounce. They won't be any match for us. We should be back to normal by then. If not, I'll do a reversal spell."

Harriet nodded slowly and held her fingertips together like a steeple, tapping her pointers in a slow rhythm. "You are positively genius. I love it."

"I'll let the set up slip with Fuzzle once I question him and then I'll go back and somehow plant the seed with Ginger Cuddlecane. You do the same with Winter and Pinecone." Harriet nodded. "Make sure you are really convincing. Trixie will be in her house, alone, checking the list at three o'clock. Got it?"

"Sure do." The gleam in Harriet's eye matched the exhilarated expression on her face.

"After you're done with Winter and Pinecone, can you pay a visit to the trusty safety officer Noel and borrow one of his cameras? That way, we can get all the evidence we need on film. I'm sure with your acting skills you'll have him eating out of your hand in no time."

"Consider it done." She held her chest high, flicked her long black hair over her shoulder and flounced toward the toy factory door. "See you back at Trixie's within the hour."

She disappeared through the door, leaving me to deal with the rush of anarchy taking over my stomach.

CHAPTER TWELVE

A euphoric rush of adrenaline hit my system as I looked at Fuzzle Bustlemitton, who was standing with his back to me in the corner of the packing room. From where I stood, he looked intimidating and downright scary. That could also be because he's taller than me and almost twice my size. If I were my real self, I could take this guy with my eyes shut.

By the time I wangled my way past every elf who wanted to put in their two cents' worth and say how amazing Trixie is, it was at least fifteen minutes since I entered the factory. Trixie sure had a lot of admirers and none too shy about wanting to have their say for the *Santa's Source*.

If only I were a real reporter, I'd make Trixie shine in the eyes of the entire village, especially Santa and Mrs Claus.

I cursed the butterflies in my belly, flipped open my notebook and tapped my pencil on the blank page. "Excuse me, are you Fuzzle Bustlemitton?" It was still weird hearing my squeaky elf voice as I spoke.

He spun and my breath caught in the back of my throat. His thick, black, bushy brows, void of any shaping, almost hid his heavy forehead creases. They reminded me of two chunks of fake fur super glued to his face. Their bushiness matched his shaggy hair. His complexion was unusually dark for an elf who lives in the North Pole where it snows all year round. He stared at me with his unsettling, rustic brown eyes and his thin lips were more like a grimace than a smile.

"Are you Fuzzle Bustlemitton?" I asked again, ignoring the continuous rolling of my stomach.

He folded his arms across his chest, stuck his chin out and the corners of his mouth turned down into a sour expression. "Who wants to know?"

"My name is Evelyn," I said with my best cheery disposition, and held my hand out. His gaze dropped to my hand, and he huffed, crossing his arms tighter.

Talk about Mr Grumpy.

"I'm doing a story on the Elf of the Year, Trixie Snowball for the *Santa's Source* and I'm chatting to all the other finalists and her friends to get the best possible picture of the winner."

His bushy brows shot up and down as if being controlled by puppet strings. Quite odd, really.

"If you want the best picture of the winner…you're looking at him. Trixie is great and all, and a real trooper, but this was my third year as a finalist and it really should have been me who won."

"Wow, third year." I slyly dropped my focus and pretended to take notes. Still, I kept one eye watching for any out of the ordinary behaviour. "Sounds like you're a bit bitter Trixie won and you didn't."

He paused and stood staring at me as if I were invisible, a vacant look in his gaze.

"Bitter…No. Upset…Yes." He took a seat beside his packing station and I followed, occupying the empty seat next to him. He continued, his eyes downcast.

"I guess I was a little upset being so close to winning and then being beaten by Trixie and Butters, but Santa has the final call and I respect his decision."

His body sunk and his shoulders cowered forward. Suddenly, he didn't seem so big after all.

"Would you say Trixie was a worthy winner?"

He nodded, but his gaze remained downcast. "Yes, of course. She'd earned the title fair and square. She scored top of the final exam, which was one of the determining factors and displays exceptional elf qualities. I guess I was just a bit bummed I couldn't match her in the rankings. She's a hard worker and…"

"And?" I prompted, scribbling gibberish as he spoke.

"I really like her," he said, biting his lip and looking shyly away.

I smiled. "That's nice."

"That's nice?" he said, an octave higher , His eyebrows shot up and his gaze found mine. "I tell you I *like her* and you say that's nice?"

The meaning of his words dropped like a bowling ball crashing to the floor. Heat flushed my cheeks and warmed my pointy ears. "Oh, you like her as in 'like' her, as in more than a friend."

He nodded. "Yes. Like I'd have a chance with someone like her. She's way out of my league."

I did not see that one coming. Trixie has an admirer. I wonder if she knows? She never mentioned it, but she has had more important issues on her mind, like finding a lost list, a murderer, and saving Christmas.

Focus, Evelyn. Over the balcony, a familiar dark-haired elf in a white lab coat and hard hat caught my attention. Ginger Cuddlecane.

Time is wasting. Check his alibi, plant the seed, and get the hell out of here.

I shuffled in my chair and refocused. "I'm sure Trixie is a good judge of character. And I would think you have just as much chance with her as any elf. I bet you were glad you didn't get caught up in the dispatch disaster yesterday afternoon."

His forehead creased, turning his bushy brows into a monobrow. "What disaster?"

"Apparently someone screwed up and printed double labels and it took all afternoon and into the evening to fix." I kept my voice monotone, but my insides were fluttering like a swarm of butterflies having a party. "Were you around to help out?"

"Me?" He shook his head. "No, thank goodness, sounds like it was a bit of a nightmare. Thankfully, I was on the morning shift yesterday and left at two o'clock."

"What did you do after work?"

"Why is what I did after work relevant to your article?" he snapped.

Oh crap.

I licked my lips and my insides turned into an all-out frenzy. "I was just wondering because I know even though Trixie's shift had finished, she said she was hard at work offering an extra hand where ever it was needed. So I thought maybe all the finalists did the same."

Fuzzle grunted, stood, and moved over to his station, and picked up a clipboard. "We can't all be as perfect as Trixie, can we? That's what makes her so likeable. If you must know, I was working out alone in my gym at home from when my shift finished until about five-thirty in the afternoon, then had dinner…with my mother. She lives upstairs, but she leaves me to work out alone. You can't get shoulders this size by lifting Santa sacks full of presents one month out of the year."

So…no strong alibi? Unless you count his mother, who may or may not have been home.

I nodded and tapped my pencil against my cheek, pretending to admire his bulky shoulders. "No, I suppose you can't." He'd be strong enough to overpower someone like Butters, and he didn't have a solid alibi.

I stood and tucked my notepad into my jacket pocket. "I can see I'm keeping you from your work. Thank you so much for taking the time out to talk to me. I'm organising a little get together for the finalists tonight at Trixie's house around seven-ish. If you're free, I'd love for you to join us. I know Trixie will be at home doing one last check of the list at three o'clock before hand-delivering the list to Santa and then we'll all arrive around six-thirty in time to celebrate. Do you think you can make it?"

"Wouldn't miss it for the world," he said, standing tall with a blank expression. "Now I must get back to work."

"Of course." An electric shiver ran up my spine and I turned and headed downstairs toward the dispatch floor. With each step I could feel my shoulders burn with his gaze drilling into my back.

When I reached the floor, the familiar whirling buzzing of a forklift at the other end of dispatch skyrocketed my pulse. After the last run in with Noel, I wasn't about to let history repeat itself. I spotted a rack of hard hats and pink safety vests hanging off to the right. Perfect.

Donning the correct safety gear, I trotted over to Ginger, remembering to maintain my cover as a newspaper reporter. "Excuse me, but are you Elf of the Year finalist, Ginger Cuddlecane?"

She spun, looking pristine in her lab coat. "Yes, I am. Can I help you?"

I planted a cheesy grin on and continued. "I'm E…Ellie and I'm doing an article on Elf of the Year, Trixie Snowball and how she interacts with all the finalists. To celebrate her achievement, I'm throwing a little party for her this evening at seven at her place. We'd love for you to attend. You know how busy Trixie is and all. I mean, she's even planning to do one last check of the list at three o'clock before hand-delivering it to Santa."

Her brow creased and her head tilted in a questioning expression. "What time did you say?"

"Seven, but you can arrive any time from six-thirty. That should be plenty of time for her to check the list, deliver it to Santa and get back in time to let loose and party."

Ginger shrugged. "Why not? She beat us all out for the top honour, so why not celebrate it? I, of all people, know how much work goes into being a finalist, let alone taking out the title. I'll be there." She turned and picked up where she left off a moment ago.

Pleased with myself, I hung my vest and hat on a hook and high-tailed it out of there back to Trixie's house. It appeared transforming into an elf had worked a treat with Fuzzle and Ginger. Even the elves that passed me in the street had no idea who I was.

I breathed a sigh of relief as I closed Trixie's front door behind me butting my back up against the hard wood.

"Thank goodness that's over." Harriet bounded out from the kitchen. The real witch Harriet that is, followed by Trixie.

"So? How did it go?" Harriet asked, eyebrows raised.

I was just about to answer when an iciness the likes I've never felt before chilled me to the core. I clutched my chest and gasped, cold air shooting from my mouth. Am I sick…or worse, dying? The horrified expression on Harriet's face frightened the hell out of me.

What in God's name is happening?

"It's okay," Harriet said. Moving over, she grabbed my elbow and guided my shaky legs to the couch.

"It's just the spell wearing off. It only takes a few seconds. I thought I was going to die until I realised what was happening."

I sat on the couch and a lightning bolt of energy shot through my entire body as if I'd put my finger in a power point. A final ripple of heat worked its way from my toes up to the top of my head, leaving in its wake a warm glow.

"Woah." I dropped my head in my hands and sucked in a few deep breaths.

"You're back," Trixie squealed and hugged me.

I looked up at Harriet from under my hooded lashes. "Next time, remind me to read up on all the details of a spell before I use it, so I know what to expect."

"Have you never used that spell before?" Trixie asked.

"I have, but on others, never on myself." I shook off the final remnants of the cold chill and turned to see Harriet munching on a bowl of Hope's trifle. "How did it go with Winter and Pinecone?"

"Like clockwork," she said around a mouthful. "I set the wheels in motion and if it's one of them I'm sure we'll see an appearance. Borrowing a camera from Noel was a piece of cake. Winter has the best job grooming the reindeer. They're so cute, and you know, Rudolf really does have a red glowing nose."

Trixie huffed and rolled her eyes. "Well, of course he does. I wish everyone would take him seriously. You're as bad as the rest of the reindeer."

"Hey, no fair," Harriet said. "I happen to think Rudolf is the smartest reindeer there is. I mean, if it wasn't for him and his bright nose, how would Santa see where he was going?"

I rolled my eyes and smiled at Trixie's cheeky grin. "How indeed?"

Harriet munched another mouthful and continued. "I've set the camera up pretty much hidden behind Trixie's Christmas tree with a clear view of the room so it should record everything. Winter has no concrete alibi for the time of death and said she went for a walk after work and then home to wrap extra Christmas presents to go to the children's home. I clued Trixie in on your plan and she's good to go. We were just waiting for you to return."

Trixie smiled and gave me a wink. "Genius plan if I do say so myself, Evelyn. I hope it works."

"It will." Gosh, I hope I haven't given her false hope. "You know, you're very popular with the elves, some more than others. As soon as word spread that I was doing an article on you for the *Santa's Source*, elves flocked to tell me how amazing you are." I watched Trixie process what I said, and she looked completely shocked. "Why does that surprise you?"

She shrugged and pulled the couch cushion into her lap, her fingers fiddling with the frilly edging. "I guess I haven't had a chance to think about it with the list going missing and then what happened to Butters and you finding the medallion and all."

I reached over and eased my hand over hers and squeezed. "I understand but know you do have a load of supporters out there."

Harriet licked the final sliver of chocolate from her spoon and dropped it in her empty bowl. "I think we should make sure everything is ready to go for three o'clock, don't you?"

I jumped at the unexpected jungle jangle of the doorbell.

Oh no, not Mrs Claus again?

CHAPTER THIRTEEN

"Please don't tell me that's Mrs Claus with more of Santa's clothes to mend?" I said, my heartbeat still racing inside my chest. "That's all we need, someone to knock on the door right in the middle of the set up and spoil everything."

Trixie opened the door and my pulse calmed slightly at the sight of Hope's red bouncy hair. Her gaze lifted and my gut tightened. No longer was she a vision of positive energy, but now she screamed distress in a teary, blubbering mess.

"Hope? Oh my gosh, what in the name of Christmas candy is wrong with you?" Trixie asked, shooing her inside and onto the couch.

"It's awful, just awful." She blew her nose and I cringed, my eardrums just about exploding from the ghastly sound. How can someone so petite make such a horrible noise? "I came over as soon as I saw it for myself."

"Saw what?" I asked, joining her and Trixie on the couch.

Hope looked at each one of us in turn and then let out a gasp. "You mean to tell me you don't know?"

"Know what?" Harriet asked, throwing her hands up in the air and flopping down on the opposite couch.

"O-M-G. Someone tried to kill Fuzzle Bustlemitton. They tried to poison him." Her eyes animated as she spoke.

"No way," Harriet muttered. "I guess he won't be showing up later."

"How can that be?" Trixie asked.

"I can't believe it." I shook my head, Hope's words spinning in my mind. "I was over there not long ago, and he seemed perfectly fine to me."

Hope paused and wiped her watery eyes with a tissue. "And that's not the worst part."

Harriet froze momentarily and then shook her head. "Wait a minute. You're saying there's something worse than someone trying to poison you?"

"No." Hope sniffed back tears and blinked a few times. "I admit, that's pretty bad. What I'm saying is what they found in his hand is the worst part."

"What did they find?" Trixie's shaky voice held no lies

She was as nervous as me to find out what was in Fuzzle's hand.

Hope turned to face her best friend. "Your gold 'T' necklace, Trixie. You know, the one I gave you for your last birthday."

Trixie's eyes widened and her jaw fell open. She gasped and her hand covered her mouth. Silence drummed all around the small house. She finally found her voice. "How can you be so sure it was my necklace?"

"Apart from the fact that I gave it to you, it has your initials engraved on it and the candy red ruby in the centre of the T. I saw it with my own eyes."

"Oh." Trixie's eyes dulled.

"Yeah…Oh is right. Someone really wants you out of the picture."

Harriet looked at Trixie and was quick to add. "If he had your necklace in his hand, doesn't that mean Fuzzle was the one who broke into your house to get it?"

My head pounded with all the scenarios rushing through my mind. "Yes, maybe."

Hope frowned. "What do you mean 'maybe?'"

"Well, yes he could have been the one, or someone planted it on him. I'm leaning towards the latter and I'm guessing it was the person who tried to poison him. Maybe they wanted to divert suspicion from themselves."

"So where do we go from here?" Hope asked.

"I'm glad you asked." Harriet said, a warm glow enhanced her rosy cheeks. "I admit this Fuzzle incident is a minor setback, but Evelyn has come up with a genius plan that is sure to catch the perpetrator."

I held up my hand and paused Harriet. Her total confidence in my plan had me wishing I could disappear and return when it was all over.

"There are no guarantees here. We can only set the trap and hope they take the bait."

"It's better than doing nothing," Harriet said. She looked at Hope, then Trixie, then tapped her chin with her finger. A classic Harriet thinking pose. "Trixie, did you manage to adjust Santa's pants?" Trixie nodded. "Evelyn, what if Hope takes Santa's pants back to Mrs Claus?"

Trixie bolted off the couch toward the neatly folded red velvet pants on the kitchen bench. "Perfect idea. Will you do it, Hope? Return these to Mrs Claus and if you happen to stop and chat for a while that would be okay too."

"Sure, happy to help."

Trixie's smile beamed as she handed off the pants to Hope. "It would be a good idea to stay away from my house for the next hour and a half at least. If Evelyn's plan has any chance of working, we can't have any interruptions and that includes unexpected visits from Mrs Claus or anyone looking for me for that matter." She snapped her fingers and slapped her leg. The sparkle in her eye lighting her smile. "I've got it. Why not ask Mrs Claus what she's cooking Santa for his Christmas Eve dinner? She always loves to talk about it and then when we know it's safe, we'll contact you there."

"If that's what you need me to do, count me in. It's the least I can do." Hope stood and gave her best friend a hug. "Please be safe, Trixie. You're my best friend in the whole entire universe and if anything happened to you, I don't know what I'd do."

Trixie nodded and the pain in Hope's eyes guttered me. I swallowed the lump in my throat. "Hope, I promise Harriet and I will do our best to make sure nothing happens to Trixie."

"And I'm not exactly a wimp either. I can take care of myself," Trixie said, making a pretend karate pose to lighten the mood.

Hope paused at the door and looked over her shoulder. "I'll be with Mrs Claus until I hear from you. Good luck." The door closed with a resounding thud and my pulse raked up ten notches.

I glanced at the worried expression on Trixie's face. Had I pushed her too far and her nerves were getting the better of her?

"Are you sure you're up to this, Trixie? We can always find another way."

She shook her head and breathed in a few fresh breaths of air, her shoulders rising with each.

"No, it's time we find out once and for all who is behind this. And if no one shows at three, I guess I was wrong and then my only option is to tell Santa and Mrs Claus everything."

"Let's hope it doesn't come to that," I said. "It might be a good idea to run through the plan one more time. Apparently, elves don't feel the need to lock their doors so we can leave both front and back open without arousing suspicion."

Harriet took over explaining with detailed precision. "You will be sitting at the kitchen bench with your back to the door pretending to check the list while Evelyn and I will be hiding behind the half-closed door leading to your study. The video camera is set up behind the tree and will get it all on tape. We'll be able to see everything."

Trixie gave a half-hearted smile and nodded, her fingers picking at her fingernail beds.

I ignored the empty stab in my stomach. "We'll be here the whole time and we will have you in our sights. You will never be alone. We're not going to let anything happen to you. If they turn up, your main goal is to make sure you get them to confess to trying to steal the list and why. And if you can get them to confess to murder, that would be an added bonus."

Harriet ran her hand through her hair. "I hate to be a buzz kill, but we need to set the recorder and disappear and Trixie needs to plant herself at the kitchen bench. We've still some time until it hits three, but for all we know, they could be early."

Harriet was right. A rolling wave of tension turned my stomach inside out. I engulfed Trixie in a heart-felt hug before moving toward the camera. "Good luck, and remember we'll be just behind that door."

"Gotcha." She gave Harriet a warm embrace. "This will work. It has to," she muttered as she headed toward the kitchen bench.

It was after three and I was about to give up hope all together when I heard a strange ruffling sound by the front door. I kept my eye glued on Trixie and her back stiffened.

She heard it too. Looks like it's show time.

"I think someone's here," Harriet whispered, her hot breath tickling the sensitive skin behind my ear. I nodded. A bead of sweat ran down my temple when I nodded. I cannot believe I am sweating, and in the North Pole, of all places.

My eyes stung as I stared at the door, waiting to see who'd walk through. A familiar stocky figure emerged and although I couldn't see their face, there was no mistaking the straight raven black hair tightly pulled back into a slick ponytail. She may not be wearing her white preppy scientist coat, but there was no mistaking her gorgeous figure. My hand flew to my mouth, blocking a gasp.

Ginger Cuddlecane? Are you serious? What was all that talk about working flat out in a disaster?

I held my breath as she edged her way into the room, her focus solely on Trixie's back. My heart jumped into my throat as she sat there seemingly oblivious to her advances. Trixie spun, and I stood frozen at the look of horror on her face.

"Ginger Cuddlecane?" Trixie muttered in shock. "I don't believe this. Why Ginger? You of all elves. I never would have picked it in a million elf years."

She grunted and withdrew an object from her back pocket. She held it out, and Trixie's sharp intake of breath matched mine. A letter opener in the shape of a sword.

"Just give me the list, Trixie. I have no desire to hurt you. I just want the list." She edged her way around the coffee table and Trixie slid off the chair slowly moving around the other side of the kitchen bench. List or no list, she held her hand behind her back as if she had one.

"Why would you want to steal the list?" she asked.

Damn it, she's cornered herself in the kitchen with no escape. My galloping pulse rate shot through the roof.

"Give me the list, Trixie." She had a sinister edge to her tone that sent shivering goose bumps up my arms.

"But you had an alibi," Trixie pleaded.

"I know. That's what you were supposed to think." She let out a sinister witchy laugh that had my blood curdling. "Pfft, those dummies had no idea what was going on. *I* was the one who orchestrated the double label printing in the first place so all my crew would have to stay back and provide me with an alibi. That is what's good about being the boss. You can delegate and wreak havoc so everyone is too busy and worried about what they're doing to watch what I'm doing."

"You're one of the smartest elves I know. You've always been top of the class and you excel at everything you do. The least you can do is tell me why," Trixie snapped.

"Exactly," she roared. "I excel at everything, that is until you decided to run for Elf of the Year. Failure is not an option for me."

Trixie shook her head. "Coming third is hardly a failure."

"It is in the eyes of my parents. I would have won and then you came along and made the final six. You have to be so perfect, don't you? This year was *my* year to win…*my* year to be the elf that gets it all. I worked my butt off to get where I am, and this was going to take me all the way. But then who can compete with perfect Trixie Snowball, sure as hell not me. Just give me the list Trixie, I really don't want to hurt you."

Trixie frowned. "I don't get it."

She huffed and her shoulders shook as she laughed in Trixie's face. "Of course, you don't, why would you? You see the good in everyone. Thanks to a few bad decisions on my part, I made the naughty list this year, and if I want any chance at qualifying again next year, I can't let Santa see that list."

Trixie paled, and I almost bolted out from my hiding place to help, but I held my ground until she could get a confession.

Her eyebrows creased. "*You* made the naughty list, but how?"

"I cheated, okay?" she blurted. "I cheated on the final elf exam. The pressure to win got to me and I thought I had all my bases covered, but one little mistake and I get pushed over to the naughty list. That's why I have to destroy the list before Santa can see it."

"That's crazy. You can't tamper with the list," Trixie said, in an elevated pitch. "It's against elf law."

"Can't I?"

She took a step toward her and I flinched. Trixie recoiled, keeping the distance between them. "And what about Fuzzle? Did you try and kill him too?"

She threw her head back and laughed. "He was getting too close. After your visit this afternoon, he started asking too many questions, so he had to go. I'd killed once, why not do it again? My life will be ruined if that list gets to Santa."

"What about Butters' life? What did he ever do to you? Did you strangle him with my dressing gown belt?" she asked, a quiver of sadness in her tone.

The growing agitation in her voice sent off alarm bells in my gut. I glanced at Harriet and she nodded in agreement.

"Butters was just as slippery and slimy as his name indicated." Ginger barked out the words. "Everything would have been fine had he not caught me in your house looking for the list. That creep was going to blackmail me. Blackmail me of all people. He said he could get his hands on the list, but it was going to cost me. I wasn't about to be blackmailed by that no-good conniving elf. It would never stop, and I'd be the one answering to him for the rest of my life. And if my parents found out, I'd be disowned for sure."

Trixie's shoulders heaved as she processed her words. "So, you murdered him and dumped him in Saltwater Cove?"

She shrugged her petite shoulders. "Why not? You're the one who has links to that place, not me. It will just look like you lost the list and then killed Butters in a fit of rage when he confessed he was going to tell Santa and Mrs Claus the truth. Once I had your dressing gown belt wrapped around his neck, he barely even put up a fight. Framing you was the easiest part of all. When you're found guilty of his murder, it will leave the top spot of Elf of the Year open for me to slot right in. Either way, you're a goner. Perfect if I do say so myself." She lunged for Trixie, plunging the letter opener toward her stomach. "Now, give me the list."

Adrenaline charged my entire body, ready to defend when needed. I whispered to Harriet, "When I say go, I'll tackle her legs and you go for the letter opener, got it?"

She nodded her understanding.

Trixie gasped and jumped out of the way. She gritted her teeth together and spat, "Over my dead elf body."

My voice screamed in my head.

No, don't do it Trixie.

"Have it your way." Ginger jumped forward and lunged for her again.

"Go," I said to Harriet as I bolted from my hiding space. I reached Ginger just in time to see a handful of Hope's trifle splat right in her face.

"Ah, you'll pay for that." She staggered and stumbled, scraping trifle out of her eyes. Taking advantage of her lapse in concentration, I dove for her ankles and her body jolted forward as it hit the ground. My ears met with the sharp fumbling clatter of metal scraping along the floor. Screams and muffled yells followed and for a second, I wasn't sure who was yelling what.

I looked up to see Harriet beaming in triumph. She had her arms pinned to her back, a sock stuffed in Ginger's mouth, and the letter opener across the other side of the kitchen floor. My head pounded as she struggled against her restraints.

Trixie stood by the kitchen bench, her jaw dropped and gaze wide. "I didn't earn Elf of the Year for nothing, you know." She raced over to her Christmas tree and pulled a string of coloured lights off and handed it to Harriet. "Here, tie her up with this. I'll call Hope and Mrs Claus. I think it's time Santa knew the whole story."

CHAPTER FOURTEEN

"**M**rs Claus, you have to believe me, I didn't do anything wrong," Ginger blubbered, tears streaming down her cheeks. "They're trying to frame me."

Is this prissy, snotty-nose elf for real?

Blood boiled in my veins and I saw red. I can't believe she's trying to wangle her way out of this. Harriet, Hope, and I stood off to the side and held back even though I wanted to make Ginger sing like a bird. She didn't realise she confessed on camera.

Mrs Claus stood in front of Ginger, two elf police flanking her. She wore a pondering expression that focused solely on Ginger. "What exactly are you saying?"

"I'm saying that I'm innocent," she blurted, practically in hysterics.

Gee, I thought Harriet was a great actress. She can't hold a candle to Ginger.

A rich red hue coloured Trixie's face and her jaw dropped. "Oh pa-lease, you have got to be kidding me." She turned to Mrs Claus and took a big breath. "She's lying through her tears, Mrs Claus."

"What?" Ginger gasped and a fresh bout of tears streamed down her cheeks. "How could you say such a horrible thing?"

"Trixie's right," I said, stepping forward. "Ginger cheated on her final elf exam. She couldn't handle striking out in front of her parents and knew she'd make the naughty list for cheating. Butters Muffinsong caught her in the act of trying to steal the list from Trixie and Ginger killed him and tried to frame Trixie by strangling him with the belt of her dressing gown. She dumped his body in Saltwater Cove. She even tried to poison Fuzzle earlier today."

Ginger paled and sobbed uncontrollably. "No, no, no." She pounded her fist on her thigh and the pitch of her voice skyrocketed. "I...Did...Not...Do...Anything...Wrong."

"Oh really," Trixie said, a sly look of victory edged the corner of her mouth. She pointed to the Christmas tree. "See that camera set up behind my Christmas tree?" She paused, and all eyes descended on the camera. "It's been recording since you took your first step inside my house. It has our whole conversation on it. Are you sure you want to stick to your story? Do you want to fill Mrs Claus in, or shall I?"

"W…what?" Ginger said, in a thick, emotion-choked voice. The whites of her eyes stood out as she raised her eyebrows, her jaw opened, then closed, then opened again.

"Like I said." Trixie paused and folded her arms across her chest. "I didn't win Elf of the Year for nothing."

Once she realised the gravity of her situation, her jaw clamped shut. Her head jerked to Trixie and her nostrils flared. "This is all your fault. Butters deserved everything he got. Why you little no-good piece—"

"That will be quite enough out of you, Ginger Cuddlecane," Mrs Claus snapped.

Her sharp tone caught everyone by surprise, including me.

"I'm pleased to report that Fuzzle Bustlemitton will make a full recovery." Mrs Claus leaned in closer to Ginger and stared deep into her eyes. "I think you'd be wise to keep your mouth shut from now on."

Elation warmed my heart as Ginger's shoulders hunched forward and she locked her lips together. I wanted to jump up and high-five everyone, but I kept my cool and hid my jubilation behind my smile.

Mrs Claus turned to the elf police on her right. "Please escort Ginger to jail where she can think about how she's going to explain her actions to Santa."

"Yes, ma'am." Ginger put up a struggle, but even she was no match for the strength of the elf police. She turned and glared at Trixie, her lip curling as they escorted her away.

"Trixie, I must say, you really have earned your title of Elf of the Year. I'm not sure it was in your job description to catch a murderer, but you did." She smiled and her pale blue eyes sparkled like the sun glistening off the ocean on a summer's day. "Christmas couldn't be in better hands."

A moment of awkward stillness fell over the room. Trixie's elated expression fell by the wayside and my heart broke as she gnawed on her bottom lip with her teeth.

I bet she's thinking of the lost list.

Trixie sucked in a deep breath, rolled her shoulders back and stepped forward. "Mrs Claus, there's something I need to tell you."

"Oh." Mrs Claus looked hopeful.

"I have to tell you—"

Hope bolted from her stationary position and flung her arm around Trixie's shoulders and squeezed. "What Trixie was going to tell you is how honoured she is to be able to set an example to all the other elves in Santa's Village and show them what it means to be Elf of the Year."

I looked at Harriet and she shrugged. What the…? What is Hope on about? She obviously knew something we didn't.

A glowing smile crossed Mrs Claus' face, and she nodded. "And she's doing an amazing job." She leaned in toward Trixie and Hope and whispered behind her hand. "Don't tell anyone, but Santa asked me who I thought the top job should go to, and you were my first pick. I guess it goes to show behind every great man is a smart woman." She stood and straightened her coat. "I'll be off now and don't worry about Ginger, I'll take care of her and notify the Saltwater Cove police."

I cleared my throat and swallowed. "Mrs Claus, be sure to contact Detective Micah Huxton at the Saltwater Police Station. He will be the best person to talk to. Tell him Evelyn and Harriet will be able to fill him in on all the details."

She nodded. "Will do. Now you all enjoy the rest of your evening. One more sleep until Christmas Eve."

Trixie stood frozen to the spot, watching Mrs Claus close the door behind her. She spun and glared at Hope. "What are you doing? I was about to—"

Hope butted in once again. "Make the biggest mistake of your life admitting you lost the list."

"What are you talking about?" Trixie asked folding her arms across her chest. "I *have* lost the list."

A twinkle sparkled in Hope's eye. "I wouldn't be so sure about that."

"Wait…wait…wait," Harriet said, holding up her hands to stop the conversation mid-stream. "Is everyone confused, or is it just me?"

Trixie tilted her head back and rubbed the base of her neck. "I really have no idea what you're talking about, Hope."

"I'm talking about this," Hope said, pulling an envelope from her jacket pocket and handing it to Trixie. "When I was chatting with Mrs Claus, she happened to mention she got this unusual letter addressed to Trixie. She thought it was junk mail and then when I asked to see it, I recognised Butters' handwriting. See?" She pointed to the front of the envelope. "That's his curly T. I don't know what's in it, but I figured it was important if he sent it via Mrs Claus. He obviously didn't want anyone else to see it. I said to Mrs Claus I'd make sure it got to you."

"What does it say?" I asked. My stomach buzzed and my fingers twitched.

The edge of the envelope shook in Trixie's hand. She lowered herself to the couch in slow motion, her eyes glued to the words on the envelope.

"For Trixie, Elf of the Year."

A knot tightened my chest. The wait was killing me. It was like waiting for one of Aunt Edie's delicious apple pies to bake in the oven before I could sink my teeth into it.

"Well…open it."

Trixie's fumbling fingers ripped it open and her eyes widened as she read. Not knowing what was written was driving me insane. I was about to jump out of my skin.

"Come on, Trixie what does it say?" Hope asked, flopping down on the couch next to her. "Stop keeping us hanging here."

Trixie swallowed and a wide grin spread across her face. "Um, he hid it all along. Butters…he hid the list. It's been here in my home this whole time."

"What?" Harriet asked.

"You're kidding," muttered Hope in surprise.

Trixie's gaze darted to her Christmas tree, and she bolted toward it, her eyes rushing over the beautifully decorated tree like she was counting a swarm of bees. "He knows how particular I am when decorating my tree." Her eyes kept counting. "He left me a clue. He wrote…What makes Christmas morning the best in the eyes of children? Twelve is a good number, but sometimes thirteen is better. Find the odd one out."

Odd one out? What on earth does that mean?

I may not know but judging by the excitement bleeding from every pore in Trixie's body, she knew exactly what it meant. Harriet, Hope, and I waited patiently, my insides vibrating with each second that clicked past.

"On Christmas morning children run to the tree to see what presents Santa has left them. In the eyes of the children it's what makes Christmas morning so special. The tree." Trixie edged her way around the back of the tree and paused. Her eyes widened, accompanied by an audible gasp. "And Butters knows my favourite number is twelve. Twelve days of Christmas. I have twelve of every ornament on my tree except…" She removed an oversize candy cane and held it out. She glowed like she'd just found a chunk of gold. "…except this odd candy cane." She ripped it in half.

No way! A USB stick hidden in the candy cane. Who would have thought?

"Woohoo," Hope yelled and skyrocketed off the couch. "Go Butters." She raised her eyes to the heavens. "Wherever you are, thank you."

Tears glistened in Trixie's eyes and my heart exploded with joy. A single tear edged the corner of my eye, but I caught it in time and wiped it from existence. I glanced at the clock and there was just enough time before the rest of the finalists arrived for Trixie to make good on her promise.

"Now you have the list, how about we deliver it to Santa before anything else happens and then we head back to Saltwater Cove where you can return to Detective Huxton what you conveniently borrowed."

In a blink of an eye, Trixie bounded over and wrapped her arms around my neck.

"Thank you, thank you, thank you from the bottom of my heart." She pulled back and her teary gaze looked between all three of us. "Thank you, all of you. You saved my bacon this year and I will never, ever forget it. You're the best. I couldn't have wished for better friends."

Harriet flicked her hair and blew on her fingernails, followed by a short sharp rub against her collarbone. "Pfft, all in a day's work."

I folded my arms, pursed my lips into a thin line, and glared at Harriet. "A day's work? I'd rather never repeat this day again if it's all the same to you."

I wrapped Hope up in a ginormous hug and squeezed. "Thank you for your help."

A raspy voice, barely above a whisper echoed over my shoulder. "Ca…can't…can't breathe."

My arms tingled, and I released Hope. "Oops, sorry. Promise me, when we're gone, you'll keep Trixie out of trouble?"

She nodded and tears glistened in the corner of her eye and my chest clamped tight. "Please don't cry otherwise this is going to be the hardest goodbye ever."

"I can't stand sad goodbyes." Wiping her tears away with the back of her hand, Hope gave Harriet and me one more hug and then headed for the door.

"I'll see you around like a rissole." Then she was gone.

I turned towards Trixie. "Now, about returning that evidence you secretly borrowed to a certain police station?"

Trixie's eyes widened and she pulled out the thin dressing gown belt from her pocket where she'd kept it securely tucked away. "You mean this?"

I tilted my head and nodded. "You know that's exactly what I mean. I think it's time to make a quick stop at the Saltwater Cove police station. What do you think?"

"Let's not forget this," Harriet said from the other side of the room.

I spun to see her standing by the kitchen bench, the small box from the dresser in her hands. "Thank you. I almost forgot in the excitement of catching Ginger." I held my hands out and Harriet surrendered the box. My hands tensed under its weight and that of the unknown future.

"Saltwater Cove, here we come." Harriet ginned rubbing her palms together. "Wait, how do we get home?"

"Leave that to me," Trixie said. She held her hands out and her palms open. I grabbed one and Harriet held the other, and we stood still for a few moments.

"Well?" Harriet said, tapping her foot. "Is something supposed to happen?"

A sparkle twinkled Trixie's eye, and she said, "I'm sure you've heard this one before. 'Twas the night before Christmas and all through the house not a creature was stirring not even a…" She paused, waiting.

Harriet and I smiled and said in unison with Trixie, "Mouse."

A familiar blinding light exploded all around me and I snapped my eyes shut, squeezing Trixie's hand. My breath caught in the back of my throat. Once again, the force of weightlessness floated my body above the ground. My mind spun for all of five seconds and then another familiar thump. My feet hit the ground with a thud. A gush of shivers vibrated from my feet up to the top of my head.

I peeled my eyes open and stood staring at the closed glass doors into the police station. "You couldn't have picked a perfect place to land."

Trixie grunted, "Time to face the music."

CHAPTER FIFTEEN

Instead of having to repeat myself a gazillion times, I waited for everyone who needed to know the story to arrive at the Saltwater Cove police station before diving into an explanation. Detective Huxton, although frustrated, agreed that it was best to wait.

Tyler was the last to arrive having come straight off another surveillance job. My throat clamped up as he walked through the station making a beeline straight for me. It's only been a day since I saw him, but my heart missed him all the same.

"Hey, Evie girl," he said, brushing a few stray strands of hair behind my ears. My skin tingled under his touch.

"Psst, hey you two."

I turned to see Harriet pointing to the roof. My heart warmed at the sight of mistletoe hanging above us.

Tyler raised his eyebrows and his gaze dropped to my lips.

"When in Rome," he said, bending down, his lips skimming mine in a delicately sensual kiss.

Oh how I've missed this man.

Detective Huxton's grumpy voice shattered my moment of pure bliss. "Now that everyone is here, do you think you could explain why I had to stop what I was working on and call a family meeting in the middle of my police station?"

Harriet giggled. "Family meeting. That's a good one."

I looked around at the many faces around the room. Aunt Edie, Harriet, Eli, Wade, Tyler, and Detective Huxton. The only one who was missing was Jordi, who was still holidaying in Australia. He was right though; we were a family.

I cleared my throat and looked at Trixie. "Let me introduce you to my friend, Trixie Snowball. She's an elf." Mutters and mumbles came from all directions. I continued, "Trixie was in a bit of a bind and Harriet and I lent her a helping hand."

Trixie stood and took over the explanation, her worried gaze moving from one person to another. "Evelyn didn't know I was an elf. I used to visit her before her parents died and she thought I was her imaginary friend. But as you can see." She paused and pulled off her beanie. "I'm 100% elf."

"Does this have anything to do with the dead elf laying on a slab in my morgue and a call I got from Mrs Claus not too long ago?" Detective Huxton asked.

Trixie nodded. "I'm afraid it does. The dead elf is Butters Muffinsong. He was runner-up in the Elf of the Year competition and I own first place. To cut a long story short, Ginger Cuddlecane, another finalist used this—" she withdrew the dressing gown belt from her pocket and held it up "—to strangle Butters and dump him in Saltwater Cove. She has some serious issues and blames me for taking her spot as winner and when Butters caught her trying to steal Santa's list, she killed him. Thanks to Evelyn and Harriet, the list is back in Santa's hands where it belongs, and Ginger is behind bars in the North Pole."

Trixie walked over and handed the belt to Detective Huxton. "This belongs to you. Please accept my apologies for taking it. It has my DNA all over it, and I knew I was being framed for his murder. I took it but promised Evelyn that I would return it once I proved my innocence."

Detective Huxton crossed his arms, squinted his eyes, and leaned in towards Trixie. "Am I supposed to be happy that you're returning evidence after illegally taking it in the first place?"

She shook her head. "No sir."

"Oh Micah," Aunt Edie said, swatting him on the knee. "You're scaring the poor elf half to death. She owned up to her mistake and is confessing in front of all of us. Don't you think that's punishment enough?"

Aunt Edie's banter eased the built-up tension in my neck and shoulders I'd been holding onto since I arrived back. Detective Huxton really was a big softy at heart.

"I suppose we could call it case closed," he said, popping the belt in an evidence bag and then in his top draw. "I mean it's not every day you get a call from Mrs Claus herself explaining the situation and vouching for the integrity of the Elf of the Year."

Trixie beamed from ear to ear as did the rest of us. "Thank you, oh thank you sir and I promise this year, Santa will have something special in his big red bag just for you."

He chuckled and glanced over at Aunt Edie who was sitting in the chair beside him. "I've got all I need this year but thank you for the gesture."

She nodded and shook his hand. "I'll hand over to Evelyn now. I think what she has to tell you all will be far more exciting."

After I cleared my throat, I tapped a hand against the side of my thigh unsure where to start. Tyler tensed beside me and my face burned under the many sets of eyes focused my way.

"It's Salis, isn't it?" Eli asked. "As soon as I walked in the station, I could sense something was off with you."

"Is this true, Evelyn?" Aunt Edie asked, the concern in her expression tore at my heart.

"Yes and no."

"What's that supposed to mean?" Detective Huxton rubbed his chin. "Enough with the riddles, Evelyn. Give it to us straight."

"Okay," I said, pulling back slightly, my hand pressing against my hardened stomach. "While in the North Pole, Harriet stumbled across a box that was given to Trixie by my mother the year before they were killed." I paused, sensing the pain shooting from Aunt Edie's broken heart. She knew straight away I was feeling the same hurt and loss she was.

It's okay, love, you must continue. I'll be okay, we all will.

Aunt Edie, hurting you is the last thing I ever wanted to do.

If our life is ever to be normal again, we must know all there is to know about the Sphere and Salis.

Wade's brows drew together, and his gaze darted from Harriet to me to Aunt Edie, almost like he was watching a tennis match.

"Someone want to fill me in?"

"Pfft." Harriet swished her hand nonchalantly. "You get used to that. Aunt Edie and Evelyn chatting telepathically, I mean."

"I think it would be best if all conversations are spoken out loud for all to hear. Especially if it has a direct link to what's been happening in Saltwater Cove over the recent months with the sale of illegal spell ingredients on the black market." Wade's stern voice grated on my nerves.

"It doesn't," I piped up, keeping my gaze firmly on his. "But I'll be sure to keep your suggestion in mind." It was time to get this over and done with and get back to celebrating Christmas with the ones I love. "In the box I found a handkerchief I gave my mum and also a gold medallion with strange markings on it, sort of like Egyptian hieroglyphs. I'm pretty sure it's one of the four relics relating to the location of the Sphere."

Harriet jumped up and took over, the excitement in her voice contagious. "When Trixie and I held the medallion, nothing happened, but when Evelyn held it, it did all these strange magical things and then the words unjumbled and read; To change one's destiny, you must first discover the hidden truth. Pretty cool, huh?"

"It would be, if we knew what it meant," Detective Huxton said behind a muffled grumble.

"We will, don't you see. It's Evelyn," Trixie said with a warm smile. "She's the one who holds the answer to the mystery behind the Sphere and her parents' death. Judging by what happened when she held the medallion, it will be Evelyn who will discover the hidden truth and therefore change the destiny of the entire world."

"Ease up," I said. "This saving one's destiny stuff is getting a little too heavy for the holiday season. I'd be happy with just getting the rest of my Christmas shopping done and getting through Christmas day without any dead bodies, break-ins, or unexpected visits from elves. Who's with me?"

There was a moment of awkward silence and everyone looked around the room, then they burst into giggles and laughter. I soon followed suit and my chest warmed with love for my friends, old and new. This was going to be the best Christmas ever. I could feel it in my bones. My smile glowed.

"Merry Christmas." As if on cue, we all said in unison between giggles and laughter.

"Merry Christmas."

"And a happy new year," Wade said, his voice carrying above the chorus of laughter.

Trixie stood and headed towards the door. "That's my cue to leave." She paused and turned around and looked straight at me, her eyes shining with a fresh batch of tears. "Thank you again, Evelyn, for saving me and saving Christmas. I'll never be able to pay you back."

Harriet rolled her eyes and huffed loud enough to grab the attention of everyone in the room. "Gee, glad you were able to do it all by yourself, Evelyn."

Trixie's eyes softened and filled with an inner glow as she looked at Harriet. "Of course, I mean you too, Harriet. We couldn't have done it without your expert help."

Harriet grinned and bolted from her chair, throwing her arms around Trixie. "You're the best elf ever. I'll never forget this Christmas as long as I live, which I hope is a very long time."

"So do I," Trixie said, giving her a hearty squeeze.

"I second that," I said, my chest tightening and I looked at Eli. I nearly lost her once before, I can't let that happen again. Eli may be my Guardian, but it couldn't hurt for him to watch over Harriet as well. He nodded and the tension in my chest nudged itself loose. "Thank you," I mouthed.

"It was great meeting you all." Trixie waved at everyone. "I'm Elf of the Year, but I've a ton of work to do and the Christmas deadline is fast approaching. Don't forget to stay off the naughty list, or else…" She winked, and a tingle of happiness filled my heart.

Wade rose and moved towards the door. "Wait up Trixie and I'll walk you out. I'll take my leave now too and head on home and write up this report."

"Good work, Wade." Detective Huxton nodded. "Be sure to have it on my desk first thing in the morning."

"Of course. Thank you, sir. Have a merry Christmas everyone."

My shoulders slumped, exhaustion taking over every inch of my body. "You know what I want for Christmas?" I said, my head resting on the back on the chair.

"I have no idea," Aunt Edie said, followed by a shrug from Detective Huxton.

Harriet squeezed her hands together and her eyes thinned. "Give me a hint and I'm sure I'll guess it."

Tyler opened his arms and winked. "Me?"

Oh, how I love my family.

"I want to get through Christmas day and the new year without one dead body turning up, without a disaster that requires me to use my magic. Just one Christmas day where I can stay in my pyjamas until midday and relax with my family and friends while stuffing my belly full of Aunt Edie's delicious food."

Harriet clapped her hands and nodded. "That sounds like the best Christmas ever. Although, to make it perfect, there would have to be the addition of some presents. You can't have Christmas without presents."

A chorus of cheers went up in agreement, filling the room with happiness.

Aunt Edie stood, her sophisticated presence commanding the attention of the room. She looked from one person to the next, her expression beaming and her cheeks glowing a rosy red.

"I propose a new tradition. We celebrate the new year in style starting this year and you're all invited. A delicious lunch banquet at The Melting Pot fit for a king whipped up by yours truly in honour of family and friends, old and new."

"I couldn't think of anything more perfect." Detective Huxton reached for her hand and wrapped his palm around hers. "I think that is the best way to bring in the new year."

"Count me in," Harriet giggled. "And Jordi when she gets back. We can't forget our favourite shapeshifter."

"Do I fall into the friends or the family category?" Eli asked.

"The jury's still out on that one," Tyler said, giving him a stern, don't-mess-with-me look. Eli's eyes widened and his mouth opened with a gasp.

"Pfft," Aunt Edie said. "Don't listen to a word he says, Eli. You're family. Anyone who would give their life to protect my niece is most definitely family."

"In that case, bring on New Year's Day."

CHAPTER SIXTEEN

I flopped back in my chair and rubbed my oversize stuffed belly, smiling across the table at Aunt Edie. "That has to be the best New Year's Day dinner ever. I think this new tradition is going to be one of my favourites."

"I couldn't agree more," Detective Huxton said, his eyes glowing as he looked at his fiancée, Aunt Edie. They locked gazes and it was as though Tyler, Harriet and I were invisible. My chest filled with warmth knowing Detective Huxton would always look out for Aunt Edie.

"Seriously?" Harriet said, breaking the comfortable silence. "When are you two going to set the date for your wedding?"

As though on cue, both Aunt Edie and Detective Huxton turned to look at Harriet. The twinkle in Aunt Edie's eye sent goose bumps dancing over my forearms.

"You're holding out on us. I can tell."

"Have you already set the date?" Tyler asked.

A cheeky giggle escaped Aunt Edie's lips and she shook her head.

"No, not yet, but we are getting close. I've narrowed it down to three possibilities."

A unified, "Three?" bellowed out across the room.

"Yes, three. It's no use rushing these things and Micah is prepared to wait for as long as it takes to get it right."

"Whoa, hold up there," Detective Huxton said, pulling back in his chair. "I may have said something along those lines, but I'd like it to be sooner rather than later."

"Here, here," I said, holding up my wineglass.

Harriet shuffled forward on her chair, a sparkle in her eyes.

"Come on, Aunt Edie, don't leave us hanging."

A sheepish look crossed Aunt Edie's face and then it was as though her eyes danced and sparkled. "How about Micah and I discuss it and—"

Before she could finish, the soulful voice of *Tones and I* blared from the counter next to the fridge. All gazes turned to the interruption and paused.

My gut tightened, and I brushed my hand aside annoyed by the intrusion.

"Whoever that is can wait. Finish what you were saying, Aunt Edie."

Harriet's back stiffened, and she gasped. Her eyes glazed over as she stared straight ahead gripping the edge of the table.

"Harriet, what's wrong?" Tyler asked, his eyes laden with concern.

A heavy weight clawed at my chest. "She's having a vision." I placed a hand lightly on her forearm and whispered, "It's okay, Harriet, work through it. You're safe at Aunt Edie's place."

Aunt Edie rose and swiped the phone off the counter. "It's Jordi."

"Hello Jordi, how nice to hear from you. Happy New Year," Aunt Edie said, keeping her gaze fixed on Harriet.

Harriet let out one almighty gasp and dropped her head, her hands pressing against her temples and her breathing laboured.

"What did you see, Harriet?" Detective Huxton asked.

"Yes, of course Evelyn is here. Is everything okay?" The haunting tone in Aunt Edie's voice sent the hairs on the back of my neck standing on end.

What is going on?

I sat with a reassuring hand on Harriet's forearm and held the other out for the phone. "Jordi, what's wrong? Are you okay?"

"Evelyn, am I glad to hear your voice," Jordi said, desperation piercing each word.

"Talk to me, Jordi. Tell me what's going on," I said, my mind racing to the worst possible scenario. "The moment your call came through, Harriet had a vision. I may be a graduate witch but that is a little too coincidental if you ask me."

"Evelyn, I need your help. I don't know what to do and you're the only one I can turn to. You have to help me. Please."

"Slow down, Jordi. Listen, Aunt Edie, Detective Huxton, Tyler, Eli and Harriet are all here so I'm going to put you on speaker phone, okay?"

"Okay."

I placed the phone in the centre of the table for all to hear. "Right, now tell me what has happened to get you so upset."

"It's your parents, isn't it, Jordi?" Harriet blurted out of the blue.

"Yes, did you see them? Do you know where they are?" The shaking in Jordi's voice did not go unnoticed.

"Wait a minute." Detective Huxton held his hand up, pausing the conversation. "You're going to have to start from the beginning, Jordi."

"My parents are missing."

Cold chills raced through my body. "What do you mean 'missing'? From the beginning, Jordi."

"Okay, but I'll give you the short version. My parents were presenting at the Shapeshifters conference this year and the conference organiser called just after Christmas and said there had been a change of plans and all presenters needed to be there by New Year. Mum and Dad left, and I followed later. They were supposed to call me when they got there, but they didn't, and now I've arrived, and no one has seen them or knows their whereabouts. I tried to find the conference organiser, but they're nowhere to be found either. You have to help me, Evelyn."

I licked my lips' trying to void my mouth of the sour taste that had invaded my tastebuds. "Help you? How?"

"You have to come to Australia and help me find them. You just have to; I can't do it by myself."

"What?" The blood ran cold in my veins.

Australia? She wants me *to come to* Australia?

"Time is running out for them, Evelyn." Harriet's voice crashed through my stupor.

192

"Did you see them, Harriet? Are they okay?" Jordi asked, almost hyperventilating.

"Yes…yes, I did and they're okay for now, but if what I saw is real, they're locked in a small room huddled in the corner. I couldn't really see it clearly, but their hands and feet were bound with duct tape."

Jordi gasped and my heart shattered. I looked at Aunt Edie and swallowed the lump in my throat. I don't know how I would survive if something happened to her.

I covered the mouthpiece of the phone and whispered, "We can't let them die. We have to do something; this is Jordi's parents we're talking about?"

There were nods all round, and we were all on the same page: Save Jordi's parents. Detective Huxton flicked his fingers as though he were brushing my hand away.

"Jordi, this is Detective Huxton. I want you to listen carefully. I understand this is distressing for you, but until we can get there, you need to stay low and out of sight. For all we know, their kidnapping could be a means to an end and you could be their target. I have a friend who owes me a rather large favour, one I'm about to cash in. Just know we're on our way."

"You can count on us, Jordi. We'll help you find your parents," Tyler said.

Detective Huxton continued, "Can you send all the information you have so far including locations and where we are to meet you through to Evelyn's computer?"

"Yes, I'll do it as soon as I hang up. Thank you. Thank you all so much." The relief in her voice lightened the darkened mood that had formed around the table. "I can't lose my parents."

Harriet shook her head. "You won't, not if we can help it. You'll have all of us, even Eli to help find them."

"Thank you all so much. I'll send through the information and see you when you get here. Bye." Jordi rang off, and the air thickened as I sat trying to comprehend how the day went from perfection to devastation in a matter of minutes.

"Looks like we're heading Down Under," Eli said.

Glancing around the table, my eyes landed on my hunky boyfriend, my thought's drifting back to my discussion with Harriet about Australia.

I don't care how hot it is, there will be no Budgy Smugglers for you, Tyler Broderick. Your sexy body is for my eyes only.

Thank you for reading **Mistletoe, Murder & Mayhem.**
If you enjoyed this story, I would really appreciate it if you would consider leaving a review of this book, no matter how short, at the retailer site where you bought your copy or on sites like Amazon and Goodreads.

YOU are the key to this book's success and the success of **The Melting Pot Café Cozy Mystery Series.**
I read every review and they really do make a huge difference.

CONNECT WITH POLLY

You can sign up for my newsletter here:
https://www.pollyholmesmysteries.com/

Keep up to date on Polly's book releases, signings and events on her website.
https://www.pollyholmesmysteries.com

Follow her on her Facebook page.
https://www.facebook.com/plharrisauthor/

Check out all the latest news in her Facebook group.
https://www.facebook.com/groups/magicmysteryromance

Check out Polly's Amazon page with links to all her current books and future releases.
Polly Holmes Amazon Author Page.

Polly Holmes Amazon Page

ABOUT THE AUTHOR

Polly Holmes is the award-winning cheeky alter ego of Amazon best-selling author, P.L. Harris. When she's not writing her next romantic suspense novel as P.L. Harris, she's planning the next murder in one of Polly's mysteries. She is a proud member of Romance Writers of Australia, Peter Cowan Writers Centre, Making Magic Happen Academy and has a Certificate in Romance Writing.

Polly's award-winning cozy mysteries are rich in storyline and location with characters that stay with you long after you turn the last page. She pens food-themed and paranormal cozy mysteries and publishes her books solely with Gumnut Press.

Cupcakes and Corpses was a finalist in the Oklahoma RWA's 2019 IDA International Digital Awards, short suspense category. *Cupcakes and Curses* claimed second place and *Cupcakes and Cyanide* gained third place making it a clean sweep in the category.

Pumpkin Pies & Potions received a 2021 Silver Titian Literary Award. Polly also won silver in the 2020 ROAR! National Business Awards in the Writer /Blogger/Author category. In the 2021! ROAR National Business Awards Polly received bronze in the Writer/Blogger/Author category and gold in the Hustle and Heart category.

Polly lives in the northern suburbs of Perth, Western Australia, with her Bichon Frise, Bella.

You can visit *Polly Holmes* at her website: www.pollyholmesmysteries.com

The Melting Pot Series

Buy links for Pumpkin Pies & Potions #1

Amazon US
Amazon AU
Amazon UK
Amazon CA

Buy links for Happy Deadly New Year #2

Amazon US
Amazon AU
Amazon UK
Amazon CA

Buy links for Muffins & Magic #3

Amazon US
Amazon AU
Amazon UK
Amazon CA

ALSO BY POLLY HOLMES

ALL POLLY HOLMES BOOKS ARE COZY MYSTERIES

The Melting Pot Cafe

Pumpkin Pies & Potions #1

Happy Deadly New Year #2

Muffin & Magic #3

Mistletoe, Murder & Mayhem #4

The Cupcake Capers

Cupcakes and Conspiracy - Prequel

Cupcakes and Cyanide #1

Cupcakes and Curses #2

Cupcakes and Corpses #3

Murder and Mistletoe #4

Dead Velvet Cupcakes #5

AWARD-WINNING AUTHOR
POLLY HOLMES

PUMPKIN PIES
& POTIONS

A MELTING POT CAFÉ PARANORMAL COZY MYSTERY #1

Witches, cats, pumpkin pies and murder!

I'm Evelyn Grayson and if you'd told me by the time I was 23, I'd have lost both my parents in a mysterious accident, moved in with the coolest Aunt ever, lived in a magical town, and I was a witch, I would have said you were crazy. Funny thing is, you'd be right.

Camille Stenson, the grumpiest woman in Saltwater Cove is set on making this year's Halloween celebrations difficult for everyone, but when she turns up dead and my best friend is on the suspect list, I have no choice but to find out whodunit and clear her name.

Amongst the pumpkin carving, abandoned houses, and apple bobbing, it soon becomes apparent dark magic is at play and I must use all my newfound witches' abilities to find the killer before another spell is cast.

Step into Evelyn Grayson's magical world in the first book of the Melting Pot Café series, a fun and flirty romantic paranormal cozy mystery where the spells are flowing, and the adventure is just beginning.

If you like witty witches, cheeky talking cats, and magical murder mysteries, then you'll love Polly Holmes' light-hearted Melting Pot Café series.

CHAPTER ONE

"Oh, my goodness, breakfast smells divine," I said, bounding down the stairs two at a time toward the lip-smacking scent streaming from the kitchen. Rubbing my grumbling stomach, I peeked over Aunt Edie's shoulder at the green gooey concoction boiling on the stove. I've been living with my aunt for the past eleven years since my parents died, and not once have I questioned her cooking abilities. Until now. I folded my arms and leant against the kitchen bench. "I know it smells amazing but are you sure it's edible because it sure as heck doesn't look like it."

Aunt Edie frowned and her eyebrows pulled together. Her classic pondering expression. She snapped her fingers and looked straight at me with her golden honey-brown eyes glowing like she'd just solved the world's climate crisis.

"Popcorn. I forgot the popcorn. Evelyn, honey be a dear and grab me the popcorn from the second shelf in the pantry. The caramel packet, not the plain."

Caramel popcorn for breakfast? That's a new one.

I shrugged. "Sure." Walking into Aunt Edie's pantry was like walking into the potions classroom at Hogwarts. Every witch's dream pantry. Normal food on the left-hand side and on the right, every potion ingredient a witch could possibly need, clearly labelled in its allocated spot. Aunt Edie would always say: a place for everything and everything in its place.

"I can't believe Halloween is only three days away," I called, swiping the caramel popcorn bag off the shelf. Heading back out, the hunger monster growing in my stomach grumbled, clearly protesting the fact I still hadn't satisfied its demand for food.

Aunt Edie's cheeks glowed at the mention of the annual holiday. "I know. It's my most favourite day of the year, aside from Christmas, that is."

"Of course." I handed her the bag of popcorn and made a beeline for the coffee machine. My blood begged to be infused with caffeine. Within minutes, I held a steaming cup of heaven in my hands. As I sipped, the hot liquid danced down my throat in euphoric bliss.

"I love how Saltwater Cove goes all out for Halloween. Best place to live if you ask me."

She paused stirring and glanced my way.

"I'm so glad you're back this year. *The Melting Pot* hasn't been the same without you. *I* haven't been the same without you."

The pang of sadness in her voice gripped my heart tight.

The Melting Pot is Aunt Edie's witch themed café. Her pride and joy. We'd spend hours cooking up new delicious recipes to sell to her customers. Her cooking is to die for, I guess that's where I get my passion from. My dream was always to stay in Saltwater Cove and run the business together, but she insisted I travel and experience the world. Done and dusted.

I glanced around the kitchen, my gaze landing on the empty cat bed in the corner. "Where is my mischievous familiar this morning? Doesn't she usually keep you company when you're cooking?"

Miss Saffron had been my saving grace after my parents died. She'd found me when my soul had been ripped out, when I had nothing more to live for.

Thanks to her friendship, I rekindled my will to live, and love.

It isn't uncommon for a witch to have a familiar. It's kind of the norm in the witch world, but none as special as Miss Saffron. My diva familiar, of the spoilt kind. Her exotic appearance with high cheekbones and shimmering black silver-tipped coat still dazzles me. They say the Chausie breed is a distant cousin of the miniature cougar. She certainly has some fight nestled in her bones. But Miss Saffron's best features are her glamourous eyes. More oval than almond-shaped with a golden glow to rival a morning sunrise.

"Oh, I'm sure she's around somewhere. She's probably found some unexplored territory to investigate. I'm sure she'll turn up when it's time to eat or you get into mischief."

Although not completely wrong, I ignored the mischief comment. "Speaking of eating, what is that?" I asked, leaning in closer, my mouth drooling at the sweet caramel aroma. A cheeky grin spread across Aunt Edie's face.

Oh no, do I want to know?

"Well, Halloween's not for everyone and some of the kids were complaining last year certain townspeople were grumpy when they went trick or treating so it got me thinking. I thought I'd spice things up a bit this year with a happy spell."

My eyebrows went up. "A happy spell?"

She nodded and scooped a little spoonful into a pumpkin shaped candy mould. "When I'm done, we'll have cheerful candy to hand out for all the grouchy Halloween spoilers out there. Within ten seconds of popping one of these little darlings in their mouth, their frown will turn upside down and they'll be spreading the happy vibes to all. I'm going to make sure this year is as wonderful as it can be."

"Aunt Edie, you can't." My stomach dropped and I gripped the edge of the kitchen bench with one hand. The disastrous implications of her words sent shivers running down my spine. "You know it's against the law to use magic to change the essence of a person. You could be sanctioned or worse, have your powers stripped."

"Relax, sweetie," she said, pausing, her smile serene and calm. "This falls under the Halloween Amendment of 1632."

"What are you talking about…The Halloween Amendment of 1632? I've never heard of it."

A subtle puff of air escaped her lips. "Halloween wasn't exactly your favourite holiday growing up, especially after your parents died, and then you missed the last two or so travelling."

"But I was back by last Christmas."

She smiled. "Yes indeed. And it was the best Christmas ever. But Halloween was always a reminder you were different."

"Yeah, a witch."

"Yes."

She placed her hand on mine. A sigh left my lips at the warmth of her reassuring touch.

"A day when young girls dressed up as witches. Where their fantasy was your daily reality."

Aunt Edie's words were like a slap in the face with a wet dishcloth. "Was I really that self-absorbed? I'm so sorry to have dumped it all on you. I guess I was pretty hard to live with at times."

"Hard? Never," she said, her jaw gaping in mock horror. "Challenging, now that's a definite possibility."

She burst into laughter and my heart overflowed with warmth as the sweet sound filled the room.

I threw my arms around her and squeezed. "I love you, Aunt Edie."

"I love you too, sweetheart."

I pulled back and drilled my eyes into hers, wanting answers. "Now, what is this Halloween Amendment of 1632?"

Her eyes sparkled like gemstones and she resumed filling candy moulds with green slimy goo. "The amendment is only active for five days leading up to Halloween and finishes at the stroke of midnight October thirty-first. It allows any graduate or fully qualified witch to enhance the holiday using magic as long as it is temporary, no harm or foul comes to the object of the spell or intentionally alters the future."

"Are you serious? That means me. I'm a graduate witch," I said. My inner child was doing jumping jacks.

Aunt Edie tutted. "True. A graduate witch who is still learning the ropes and until you receive your full qualification at twenty-five, even then, you must always strive to be the best witch you can be. We can't afford another mishap like graduation."

If it wasn't for my three besties, Harriet, Jordi, Tyler and, Aunt Edie's guidance and training, I may never have made it to graduation. My mind skipped back to the disastrous end to the graduation party. It wasn't exactly my fault the party ended in rack and ruin. Who knew having a shapeshifter for a best friend could cause so much havoc?

I caught the upturned lip of Aunt Edie and chuckled. "Oh, come on, even you thought it was funny when Jordi shifted into a raven and chased that cow, Prudence McAvoy around the ballroom. She's had it in for Jordi ever since I moved to Saltwater Cove. I guess she pushed one too many times, I mean, no-one taunts Jordi and gets away with it." I giggled, the blood-red face of Prudence covered in banoffee pie was the best graduation present, ever. "Besides, my involvement came down to wrong place, wrong time. Prudence eventually owned up, it was all on her. But I get the message. Be a good witch."

"That's my girl." Aunt Edie huffed, dropping the spoon back in the empty pan. She wiped her sweaty brow with the back of her hand and smeared the remains of the gooey green substance on her hands down her apron. "There all done. Time to let them set."

"How do you know the spell works? I mean, will they work on everyone?" I asked.

Aunt Edie crossed her arms and pinched her lips together, her cheeks glowing a cute rosy pink. "Of course, they'll work on everyone, even those beings of the paranormal kind. Since when *hasn't* one of my spells worked, young lady?"

True. You don't earn the title of master witch by doing terrible spells that fail.

She rubbed her chin and continued. "But I wouldn't say no to testing them before Halloween rolls around."

"Have you got a guinea pig in mind?" I paused at her sly grin. "All I can say is, it better not be me."

Daily life was made a whole lot easier since The Melting Pot joined Aunt Edie's house. Walking next door to work suited me just fine. Kind of like an extension of her kitchen. She loved to share her passion for cooking delicious food with the rest of the world. A passion we both shared.

I twisted my wavy blue-streaked chestnut hair into a messy bun on top of my head and shoved it under my witch's hat. Glancing at my reflection, I saw it screamed modern classy-chic witch in an understated way. My dainty black satin skirt fell just above my knees showing off my trendy black and orange horizontal strip stockings. A slick black short sleeve button-up blouse fit perfectly covered in an orange vest, the words The Melting Pot embroidered above the right breast pocket in white. To add the finishing touch, I slipped my size seven feet into a pair of black lace up Doc Martin ankle boots and tied the black and silver glitter laces in elegant bows. I surveyed my reflection one last time in the mirror and grinned. I mean, who else gets to dress up every day as a witch to go to work. "Me, that's who."

An electric buzz filled my blood as I pushed open the door and stepped into The Melting Pot, closing it swiftly behind me. A clever tactic on Aunt Edie's part to design her café like a witch's cave. Everywhere I looked shouted witch heaven. Cauldrons of various sizes and candelabras standing high on their perches framed the seating area. Pumpkins scattered among the witches' brooms and replica spell books. Potions and brews strategically placed high on display shelves gave off the perfect image of a witch's cave. Best not tell anyone they're real. Aunt Edie insisted on an element of authenticity. Every child's Halloween dream all year round. I squeezed my hands together in front of my heart. "Gosh, I love my job."

A purr echoed from the floor to my right and glancing down, I saw my four-legged feline slinking elegantly in a figure eight between my legs. "You love it here too, don't you, Miss Saffron?" She stretched and catapulted up onto the counter, her agility and poise qualities to admire. Her big yellow eyes stared at me and she purred. "I swear you know exactly what I'm saying."

Aunt Edie's merry voice trailed into the main serving area from the kitchen. "I've got a wooden spoon here dripping with the last of my famous chocolate-strawberry sauce. Unless someone comes to claim it in the next ten seconds, I'll have to wash it down the sink."

"Shotgun," I whispered in Miss Saffron's direction then took off dodging tables and chairs in record time to make it to the kitchen. "Don't you dare. You know it's my favourite."

Miss Saffron sat tall on the counter, her beady eyes keeping a firm gaze on the chocolate covered spoon in my hand. My insides salivated as I licked it clean. "Oh my God. A-MA-ZING." The best part of my childhood was beating mum to the spoon and bowl when Aunt Edie was cooking up a storm. My gut clenched. I missed my mum and dad so much some days the hurt was unbearable.

The cowbell above the main entry door jingled and I jumped, startled by the unexpected intrusion. I glanced at the antique wall clock. Eight fifteen. We weren't even open yet.

"Anybody here?" Barked a familiar grouchy pompous voice.

Great. Why does today have to start with a visit from the Queen of Complaints?

"Evelyn Grayson. Stop scowling right this instant," said Aunt Edie. "You look like you're sucking a lemon. It may be fifteen minutes before we open, but you know my policy, every customer deserves a warm witch welcome."

My chest hollowed out as Aunt Edie's words curbed my inner snob. "Of course, you're right. I'm sorry," I said, dropping the spoon in the sink and wiping the chocolate sauce from my face.

"But…" Aunt Edie paused and handed me a plate. The cheeky twinkle in her eyes confused me. "It wouldn't hurt Saltwater Cove's town grouch to be happy once in a while."

I looked down at the plate and a gasped in jubilation.

Green happy candy.

"Why Aunt Edie, you are positively sinful. I love it. But I'm not even sure a happy spell will work on Camille."

"Worth a try. After all what better guinea pig could we ask for?"

I nodded and grabbed the plate. Plastering on a smile I headed out ready to see if one happy candy can soften the most bad-tempered creature I've ever had the pleasure of meeting.

"It's about time. What does a woman have to do to get service around here?" Camille Stenson snapped. "What sort of business are you running, making customers wait so long?"

I bit my tongue and held back the cynical comment chomping at the bit to get out. "I'm terribly sorry to have kept you waiting, Miss Stenson. What can I do for you?"

Her jaw dropped and a fiery shade of red washed over her pale complexion. I pursed my lips tight together to stop the laugh growing in my belly from escaping.

"It's Wednesday or have you forgotten?" She asked, her eyebrows raised, showing the stark whites of her eyes.

A shudder bolted through my body.

Scary. Yes, I know, Mr Bain's dinner, of course.

Why he can't come in and get it himself is beyond me. She's supposed to be the loan's officer at the bank, not his wife. The sarcastic tone fuelled my inner desire to squash her like a petulant fly.

Perfect guinea pig.

I eased the plate of yummy caramel scented candy in front of Camille's nose. "My sincere apologies. Please accept one of Aunt Edie's treats as a peace offering. She made them especially for the Halloween season."

"Pfft, Halloween is a waste of time if you ask me." Camille leaned in to examine the plate and frowned. Her brows crinkled together in an unattractive monobrow. "Mmm, you're not trying to poison me, are you?"

Poison? No. Cheer you up so you can stop making everyone else miserable? Yes.

"How could you say such a thing?" I said, feigning hurt. "You know Aunt Edie's food is the best for miles around. That's why people keep coming back."

"Fine." She rolled her hazel eyes to the roof, huffed, and popped a candy in her mouth.

I stood frozen, waiting, my pulse pulverising my temples as if I was standing on the edge of a cliff ready to jump. One…two…three…four. Camille stared at me, her hazel eyes clouding over. Five…six…seven. Nothing, absolutely nothing. Eight…nine. My eye caught Aunt Edie peeking in from the kitchen and she shrugged. I guess it doesn't work on people whose core being is made up of such deep-set crankiness. Ten.

"Evelyn, my dear precious Evelyn." Camille's tone shot three octaves higher. A smile flashed across her face as electric as a neon sign in the dead of night. "You look positively radiant as always. I never seem to tell you enough how beautiful you are. Just like your mother. God rest her soul."

My mother? How did she know my mother?

I swear I'd been transported into an alternate universe. "Um, thank you. That is kind of you to say. But how…"

"Pfft, nonsense," she interrupted with a sashaying movement of her hand. "It so great to have you back in Saltwater Cove. I bet your aunt is pleased you're home?"

Did she mention my mother? Maybe I imagined it. I made a mental note to follow up Camille's comment about my mother with Aunt Edie.

"I…." Stunned by Camille's reaction to the spell, my words caught in the back of my throat.

"That I am," Aunt Edie said, threading an arm around my waist. With her head turned from Camille's view, she gave me a cheeky wink.

She handed a paper bag to Camille and smiled. "Here you go, Mr Bain's dinner. His usual, just how he likes it."

"Perfect. He doesn't know how good he has it eating your wonderful meals four nights a week. He's off to some big Banking Symposium at Dawnbury Heights this afternoon but insisted I still pick up his dinner so he can take it with him. He can't stand hotel food, mind you, who can? Makes him all bloated." Camille said, placing the food inside a bigger tapestry carpet bag.

It kind of reminded me of Mary Poppins' bottomless bag. She turned toward the exit and waved.

"Ta-ta now. You ladies have a wonderful day, and may it be filled with all the magical wonders of the world."

The cow bell rattled as she left. My jaw dropped, and I stared at the closed door in silence. I looked at Aunt Edie and within seconds we were both into hysterical fits of laughter.

"Well I'd say...that spell...is a winner, wouldn't you?" I said, barely able to speak between giggles.

She nodded and cleared her throat wiping a tear from her eye. "I hope she stays that way for the next hour and a half. But who knows, it all depends on the individual person."

I laughed so much a stitch stabbed my side. "Aw," I said, pressing against the pain. "Okay, I give up, why do we want it to last an hour and a half?"

"Because Vivienne has an appointment with Camille in about thirty minutes regarding her loan application. If all goes well, she'll be able to expand her business just like she's always planned."

Vivienne Delany and Aunt Edie have been best friends since primary school. Aunt Edie ran The Melting Pot and Vivienne was the proud owner of *Perfect Pumpkin Home-Made Treats* where she made every kind of dish out of pumpkins one could dare to conjure up. And even though they both ran food business; they'd die before letting harm come to the other. That's what best friends do for each other.

"Let hope your spell does the trick." The cow bell jiggled over the door, signalling the beginning of the morning rush. "I guess we'll have to wait and see."

Buy links for Pumpkin Pies & Potions

Amazon US
Amazon AU
Amazon UK
Amazon CA

AWARD-WINNING AUTHOR
POLLY HOLMES

DEADLY
HAPPY^NEW YEAR

A MELTING POT CAFÉ PARANORMAL COZY MYSTERY #2

Never in my lifetime did I think I'd spend New Year's Eve knee-deep in mischief, magic, and murder!

When my high-school nemesis, Prudence McAvoy, chooses The Melting Pot Café to host her New

Year's party, I know I'm courting trouble by accepting her booking. The trouble begins with Prudence turning up dead, face down in a pond, and the finger for her murder is pointed directly at my shape-shifting best friend, Jordi.

Determined to clear Jordi's name and bring the real killer to justice, I pool resources with Harriet, Tyler, and my cheeky familiar, Miss Saffron, to find out what happened to Prudence. As the clock counts down to midnight, time is running out in more ways than one.

Can we find the killer before another body drops? Or will Jordi's new year begin in the pokey?

If you like witty witches, talking cats, and magical murder mysteries, then you'll love Polly Holmes' light-hearted Melting Pot Café series.

Buy links for Happy DEADLY New Year

Amazon US
Amazon.AU
Amazon UK
Amazon CA

BOOK 3 OUT NOW

What's a witch to do when faced with protecting the ones she loves against an unimaginable evil?

Ever had one of those days when everything is going too well? When you have that sense that the other boot is about to drop? Welcome to my day.

It's the Annual Saltwater Cove Show, and this year there are more rides, show bags, food stalls, and competitions than ever before. Witches from worlds near and far have descended to try their hand at winning the prestigious Witch Wonder Trophy for best witch baker.

When Seraphina Morgan from the Coven of the Night Moon turns up dead, all avenues lead to last year's reigning champion, Aunt Edie, as the guilty party. Dark magic is lurking, and I'm determined to get to the bottom of it and clear Aunt Edie's name before the unthinkable happens, and she's found guilty. Enlisting the help of my two best friends and drop-dead Greek-god gorgeous boyfriend, we set about finding the real killer before Aunt Edie's goose is cooked. Or pie is baked as the case may be.

If you like witty witches, talking cats, and magical murder mysteries, then step into the fun and flirty romantic paranormal cozy mystery world of the Melting Pot Café series where the spells are flowing, and the adventure is sure to leave you craving more.

Buy links for Muffins & Magic

Amazon US
Amazon AU
Amazon UK
Amazon CA

CPSIA information can be obtained
at www.ICGtesting.com
Printed in the USA
BVHW081432210222
629674BV00005B/106